Modern Witches, Wizards, and Magic

Modern Witches, Wizards, and Magic
edited by Charles R. Dinkins

Copyright Acknowledgements

Cleanup on Aisle Seven, copyright 2005, Lori Ratti.

The Crystal, copyright 2005, Kathleen McCarthy

A Fool And His Honey, copyright 2000, Nick Aires.

Black Mary, copyright 2001, James Ferris

Heirlooms, copyright 2005, Albert Coelho

Encounter, copyright 2005, Mark Deloy

Black Water Bayou, copyright 2002, Stanley T. Evans

Loves Magic, copyright 2005, Donna L. Zeller.

If I Had a Hundred Tongues, copyright 2005, Barry Baldwin.

The Wish, copyright 2005, Rob Rosen.

In The Name of Desdemonia, copyright 2000, Nicholas Knight.

In The Headlights, copyright 2005, Jeannie Mobley.

My Little Elves, copyright 2005, Louise Yeiser

Lepus Europaeus, copyright 2001, Allan F. Gilbreath

The Rules of Magic, copyright 2005, Helen Grant

Minnow Slough, copyright 2001, K. Woo

CONTENTS

Foreword

Charles R. Dinkins

We all grew up with the monster under the bed or perhaps the beast that dwelled in your closet. It really doesn't matter where it came from, you knew it lurked out there in the darkness just waiting for the perfect moment to leap out and get you. As we grow up, we lose our fear of the slightly open closet door or the stuff under the bed. We also lose a bit of the thrill of the unknown. We know that nothing is going to leap out and eat us as we slumber.

Somehow that knowledge steals some of our excitement to be alive. After all, the morning looked so much more inviting if you thought there was a chance you would not live to see it. This collection of stories captures the thrill and magic of a monster under the bed and the relief of living to see the sunrise. Let go of your daily grind and allow these stories take you back to the time when spells, curses, kissing frogs, spirits, witches, monsters, and just plain surviving to see another day made life worth living.

Chuck Dinkins
October 2005

Clean Up On Aisle Seven

Lori Ratti

There is something magical about turning ten. It is that strange age that leaves you still a child but now you have left single digits behind and achieved the mystical plateau of double digits. It is the last time in your life you can hold up your hands to tell someone how old you are. Of course, it is a very long time before you can move from double digits to triple. For fraternal twins, Emily and Jasper, turning ten is even more magical because today is the day they receive their birthright.

Excited and a little jittery, they had cleaned up special today for the visit to Grandma Purdy. Emily wore her favorite pale blue sundress with her mahogany brown hair pulled back in a matching bow. Jasper had managed to find his only good pair of kaki shorts at the bottom of his closet and a short sleeve navy pullover.

They could hear their mother on the other side of the closed door. She seemed either excited or upset about something. Her voice kept rising and falling but the voice of their grandmother stayed steady. If they had been at home they would have already wandered off to amuse themselves but here, they dared not move from the ancient bench where they had been placed. Even their new portable video games sat next to them untouched.   One did not wander around this house. When Grandma Prudy said sit, you sat.

Both Emily and Jasper could sense the ornate door would be opening soon. They could just do things like that, sense that things were going to happen. Mom always told them that everyone did that but because they were twins they could do it twice as good. They did not really believe her. Mom was easy to predict. Grandma Prudy was a whole different story. They could not tell anything about what she was going to do. As a matter of fact, she usually caught them trying to catch her. That just made them more determined.

The door finally opened. Both their mother and grandmother smiled at them but they could tell that Grandma Prudy certainly seemed happier than Mom.

Mom spoke first, "Your grandmother has something for you two today."

"Something very special." Grandma Prudy added.

"I am going to leave you two with Grandma Prudy for the afternoon. Behave yourselves and I'll see you later." Mom kissed them both on the forehead then picked up her purse and walked down the hall towards the front door. Their eyes only glanced down the hall before targeting back on their grandmother. Grandma Prudy's hazel eyes absolutely gleamed with a secret. With anyone else, Emily and Jasper would have joined hands and been able to guess the secret. That trick never worked on Grandma Prudy.

"Come in here with me before the two bust." Grandma Prudy teased.

"Yes ma'am." They both chorused then obediently stood up and followed her into her study. They had never been allowed in here before. The room reminded them of their grandmother, clean and well organized if just a little overstuffed.

Two smaller chairs had been obviously set out for Emily and Jasper. A larger chair sat by closely. Grandma Prudy motioned towards the chairs and the children took their seats. The air absolutely crackled with expectation.

"So the two of you are ten today."

They both just nodded then fidgeted a bit. Grandma Prudy pulled her chair close. She looked each of them directly in the eye in turn. They looked so much alike but Emily had the darker complexion while Jasper had the curls. The children looked so innocent that there could be no doubt that they had done it, whatever it was. Both sets of deep blue eyes gleamed up at her.

"Oh yes, just as I thought. It is time we had a little talk about the family secret." Grandma Prudy leaned in even closer. "Tell me the truth now. Just what little tricks do you two already know how to do?"

"What do you mean by tricks, Grandma?" Emily asked guiltily.

"Oh my dears, you can't fool me. I know much more about the two of you than you do."

"We just kinda know stuff." Jasper confessed just before Emily did.

Grandma Prudy smiled broadly and knowingly nodded her head. "What happens when you two join hands?"

Emily grinned. "It gets easier. One time this dog kept barking at me and wouldn't go away. Jasper helped me tell it to go home and it ran away."

Jasper nodded in agreement. "We just thought about real hard."

"Would you like to know why that happened?"

"Uhh huh," in unison.

"It is because I am a witch and you sweet Emily are going to grow up a witch just like me." Emily's cherubic face absolutely lit up. She could not help shooting her brother that I have something you don't look.

"Well, that's not fair," sulked Jasper.

Grandma Prudy smiled sweetly and turned slightly to look him straight in the face. "My dear Jasper, you can't be a witch, you're a boy. Boy witches are called wizards. So here we sit, one old witch, one young witch and a precious little wizard."

Jasper beamed at not being left out. He looked at Emily excitedly and began to swing his feet.

"Now children, this is a secret that you must keep, always. There are a lot of people out there that just don't understand what you will be able to do. It may be hard but you have to promise me that this is our secret and our secret alone."

"We promise." The twins said solemnly through huge smiles.

"Now, I have something for both of you." Grandma Prudy stood and walked over to her ornate walnut writing desk. She picked up an antique looking box. She returned to her seat and held it out for their inspection. The twins stared expectantly. They nearly forgot to breathe in anticipation. Slowly, Grandma Prudy opened the lid. Nestled in the bottom of the red velvet lining lay two very elaborate gold necklaces. Each featured an amazingly clear center stone. The twins stared in amazement. The necklaces looked exactly like the perfect thing to be given right after being told you are a young witch or wizard. Each necklace exhibited the faultless combination of size, shape, and color. Each stone glistened and the center mounting looked as if it had been slowly entwined over centuries.

"Now, you can wear these all you want. You just have to keep them under your clothes." Grandma Prudy gingerly placed the necklaces over their heads in turn and helped them settle them under their clothing.

"Grandma, what do they do?" Emily asked touching the center stone under her clothing.

"Well, my little dears, they don't really do anything except to help focus your thoughts, to clarify your intent. Do you understand what I mean?"

They both shook their heads up and down in perfect unison without the faintest clue what Grandma Prudy meant. They didn't care. They had lots of cool new video games to play, a wild family secret, and bizarre new necklaces to hide from their friends. This had to be the coolest birthday they would every have.

"I thought the two of you were old enough to understand. Your mother is a little worried but I think everything will be fine." Grandma Prudy looked pleased with herself and her two grand children. "Have you had a good birthday, dears?"

"Yes ma'am." In perfect unison complete with giggles.

"Gather up your new toys. I have a hair appointment in a few minutes. When we get back, we can bake some cookies and have a little fun." The look of light mischief in Grandma Prudy's eyes told the twins that the day still held more treasures. Grandma Prudy baked the best cookies in the world. Now, they had a sneaky suspicion why her cookies always turned out so much better than anyone else's. They would have to pay special attention to everything she did. She just might give away a secret or two. They picked up their video games and followed their very special grandmother out to her car.

"Grandma?" Jasper piped up.

"Yes dear."

"We don't ride brooms do we?" Jasper asked in all earnestness.

Grandma Prudy smiled broadly. "No dear, that is all silliness on T.V. and the movies. Cars are much easier to use. Besides, I don't think a poor little skinny broom could hold your old granny."

They all snickered at her answer. Jasper giggled in relief. He had already experienced a slipped foot off of his bike pedal. That had hurt in ways he did not think he could hurt; the very thought of doing that on a speeding broom held real terror for him. Emily kept giggling at the mental image of Grandma Purdy trying to balance her girth on a skinny little broomstick. Besides, Grandma Prudy had a tendency to speed just a little so driving with her always proved to be a lot more fun than driving with Mom.

With Grandma Prudy concentrating on traffic, Emily and Jasper turned their attentions to completing the set up of their new video games. Headsets and game controllers had to be sorted out and plugged in properly. The units needs to be synched so they could either play against the game, each other, or team up for maximum destructive potential. The Kingdom of Nargur promised to pit warrior mage heroes against all kinds of hideous foes in level after level of mayhem.

Grandma Prudy managed to find a decent parking

space just about the time the game cards loaded up, ready to play. The children wrapped up their games and followed their grandmother into the megalithic building. Grandma Prudy may be a lot of very interesting things but like many people her age, she had a little difficulty grasping the new trends of the truly modern world. Malls used to be fun to shop in with lots of different stores to explore. Now, it all fits in one massive store with different departments. Whether you need a bicycle, kitchen utensils, fresh fruit, or live seafood, it is all under one huge roof. Grandma Prudy's stylist had given up her independence a few years ago and joined the Styling Department. While convenient to have everything under one roof, it was always a bit disquieting to Grandma Prudy to walk in the infrared controlled automatically opening doors, make it past the greeter, and take the hike to the side of the building where the Styling Department resided. The children had no idea the world had ever existed any other way.

The Styling Department took waiting husbands and children into consideration and provided ample comfortable seating. One could either watch the Styling Department in action, read a provided hair care magazine, or lose oneself in other pursuits. The store hoped it would be shopping.

"Now children, both of you stay right here. I'll only be a few minutes." Grandma Prudy made sure they took their seats and were more or less entrenched for the wait. "Yes, be good and play your little games. When I get done, we'll go home and I'll have some real games to teach you."

The twins giggled at the look in her eye. They had to have the coolest grandma in the world. "We will be right here."

Grandma Prudy walked to the counter only to be led back into the bowels of the Styling Department. Emily and Jasper resumed final assembly on the Kingdom of Nargur.

Emily looked and Jasper and asked, "Are you ready?"

"Yup." Jasper punched a few buttons on the tiny console. While Jasper could not have cared less, Grandma Prudy would be shocked to learn that the level of technology in the twins "little games" would have been enough to conquer the Pentagon fifteen years ago. These game consoles did not just produce cartoony characters and make squeaks and chirps. New personal hand held games, now produce near cinema quality animation with full stereo sound. Today's games are more like movies being scripted based on the players choices.

The screens lit up and began playing the sequences that explain the reason you have to save the Kingdom of Nargur. Both children sat at the ready with eyes glued to their screens and earpieces firmly in place. They didn't want to bother those around them with the sounds of their adventures. Emily selected joint play and smiled as their synchronized screens displayed their new characters, each of them splendidly decked out in oiled leather armor with lots of shiny metal bits.

Carefully, they guided their characters through the introduction level. It amounted to not much more than a simple maze coupled with the excuse to find a couple of keys they will need later in the game and it gave them a chance to get used to how the characters move and fight. With their considerable level of game playing expertise, the level did not last long. The batteries full of power and the synch working perfectly, Jasper led them into the second level. This time they encountered actual bad guys that had to beaten down with staffs and swords. The graphics made it easy to see what was coming and occasionally where it went. The sound, as real as special effects and Hollywood could make it, in a word, fantastic.

Another aspect about the greatness about being

ten is the ability to utterly lose yourself in what you are doing. While the occasional adult, mostly artist and computer types, retains the ability to lose themselves completely, the average ten year old can spend a day on Mars more easily than they can spend an hour in an arithmetic lesson. When your mind is ten years old, it still knows the thrill of new knowledge and adventure. The imagination has not yet been beaten down by tests, responsibilities, and the pursuit of the opposite gender. The mind is still fresh and growing.

Gradually, the excitement of the tiny screens and the pumping music and sounds of combat began to block out all the surrounding people, sounds, and activities. Even the Styling Department began to slip from their peripheral attention. Evil monster after monster fell before them. Level after level gave way before their dexterous fingers. Unknown to Emily and Jasper, their thoughts and intents had begun to clarify, to be filtered of outside distractions. The twins simply felt that they now played better than ever before. The amazing clear stones hidden beneath their clothes don't have to understand the difference between a game and real intent. All the stones do is react to the level of thought being poured forth from the twins, clarify and amplify.

A faint haze only visible to those with the proper eyes to see began to drift across the entire megalithic store. The up coming level of the game began to synch up with the layout of the store. If the twins had looked up, they would have been utterly amazed to see their game bizarrely superimposed over the real world of shoppers and merchandise; the walls of the castle matching the aisles of merchandise. The real shoppers now unknowingly waded through the mist of the Kingdom of Nargur.

On the tiny high definition color screens, the new level materialized. Emily and Jasper excitedly selected their weapons at hand. Emily chose the long bow while Jasper opted to be a little more up close and personal. He chose the battle-axe. Both of their athletic avatars entered the maze. Emily chose to climb a wall so she could have a panoramic view of the surrounding countryside. In the depth of the maze, she could see the advancing evil Gur platoon. They were not hard to spot in their shiny black leather armor with huge red Gur insignias in the center of their chests. With practiced deliberation, she took careful aim and let fly the deadly missile. The lead Gur made the fatal mistake of making the first turn. His body dropped like a stone. The front wheels of Rowlett Wheeler's shopping basket skidded as she pushed through the Gur's virtual mortal shell. She backup up then pushed through, smiling once the wheels straighten out.

The Gur, now alerted to Emily's presence, took cover. Her next shot went slightly high and stuck in the wall behind her target. Her earpiece let her know it with a resounding thunk. The impact of the virtual bolt transferred to the back of a jar of peaches in heavy syrup. The jar tipped out and over the rail in top stock and crashed to the floor. The security cameras that are ubiquitously present in all such stores confirmed to the guard that no had been injured or had actually been anywhere near the now stricken jar.

"Good afternoon shoppers please be aware we have a clean up on aisle seven. Clean up on aisle seven. Please enjoy your shopping experience with us." The dual-purpose announcement both alerted the staff to the mess and the shoppers to be wary in a cheery yet somehow droning voice. Three employees sprang into action. The first arrived with the broom, dustpan, and pail. The second arrived with the wet floor signs and had them appropriately positioned by the time the third employee arrived with the mop and bucket. They bent to their task completely unaware that they stood in the middle of savage Gur warriors protecting themselves from Emily's deadly missiles.

The heavily muscled avatar of Jasper crept through the maze looking for his sworn enemies. The gentle jingle of his armor, while it helped heighten his gaming experience through the earpieces, it seemed to have no effect on the shoppers he moved around and through. Jasper knew from the sound of combat that Emily had already engaged the enemy. A quick glance over his shoulder and he could see her atop a wall looking for open targets with her bow. He smiled a tight grimacing smile. All he has to do is flush the Gur out and Emily will eliminate them one shot at a time. They should blow through this level quickly.

One thing that Alfred McGuiness looks forward to every summer is the arrival of the watermelons. While his childhood ceased to be nearly sixty years ago, his memory fills his senses with the treasured experience of fresh, cold watermelon. On hot summer days, he and his mischievous compatriots would sneak into the backfields of nearby farms. There, they would find a nice watermelon and steal away with it down to the creek. They had carefully constructed a trap to hold their purloined prize in place in the cold creek water. At the end of their hot and tiring day they would return to claim their now chilled prize. Alfred looked over the stack of melons experimentally tapping one then another, listening intently for that perfect tone that only a ripe watermelon will make when properly tapped by an expert. One especially nice looking and sounding watermelon had been decoratively laid out lengthwise on a bed of crushed ice. Obviously, the department manger meant to cut this one in half to tempt the shoppers into purchasing its whole brethren.

A Gur warrior crept along a series of barrels, bags, and other storage. Frustrated at not being able to see his enemy, he stood up from his relative safety only to see a massively muscled warrior mage taking aim at him with a huge battle-axe. The Gur dove for safety as Jasper hurled his lethal weapon dead down the center. The mighty steel blade bit deeply into the stack of storage material behind the space the Gur had just hastily vacated.

Alfred had only turned away to check his basket for the briefest moment when a odd blur caught his attention out of the corner of his mind. He had no idea how he could have missed the fact that the watermelon on display had already been cut. He could now clearly see the sliced edge. Gently, he pried the halves apart and inhaled deeply. His memories thrilled to the scent of days gone by. Alfred placed the next melon that sounded right in his basket and whistled happily to himself as he continued his shopping.

Brad and Stacy had worked together in the kitchen prep area for two years. Brad fancied himself a great chef in training. With the idea of a bakery expanded to roasted meats, exotic cheeses, dozens of breads, and ready to heat and eat meals Brad enjoyed everyday he learned something new. For Stacy, this served as the second job to cover part of her daughter's tuition. Over the last year, she and Brad had hit the proverbial groove in the kitchen. Outside of a few pleasantries and the daily news from home, they rarely spoke after they agreed upon the jobs list. Their timing looked almost psychic. One prepped the food while the other set up the next round of ingredients or checked the array of mixers, ovens, and roasters. Today, the entire store would be treated to the aromatic thrill of roasted peppers. Now that grilling and western food had caught on, all things pepper had high demand. While Brad tenderly washed the huge green chillies, Stacy automatically set out the roasting pans. Brad didn't have to look for the pans, he already knew where they would be sitting. Stacy set the ovens to warming then headed for the walk-in refrigerator while Brad set the peppers out on the pans. Once loaded, Brad placed the pans on the prep rack while the ovens got up to temperature.

Emily jumped from one low wall to another until she could just see the major part of the Gur force hiding back by the cooking fireplaces. She grinned. She had just the thing for this situation. She put away her bow and reached into her mage's bag. After a moment of searching she found exactly what she wanted. She raised the oily looking ball of rags to her lips and whispered the words of power into it. She smiled broadly as the ball emolliated and burned bluely in the center of her gloved hand. Emily checked her distance again, wound up, and let fly the growing fireball. The Gur scattered as they perceived the incoming danger. Emily's flaming ball of destruction arched gracefully into the fire pits and exploded with spectacular color and other effects.

Brad waited on a couple of customers at the far end of the counter, filling their orders in his usual friendly demeanor. He only seemed to spend the extra moment with each customer. Actually, he never stopped moving the whole time he chatted with the person in front of him. Once the counter cleared, he walked back to the ovens only to be greeted with the rising aroma of roasted peppers. Apparently he had spent more time with the customers than he thought. He smiled at the finished peppers. Stacy must really be on a roll today. Brad left the freshly roasted peppers to cool. As he walked back to stockroom, Stacy rounded the other corner from the walk-in. She smiled at the sight of the peppers already done. Brad must really be on a roll tonight. He had even been thoughtful and left the ovens on for her.

Emily learned on the earlier levels to pay close attention to any sounds that did not seem to have an obvious visible source. The stray auditory sensation sounded like something being drawn taut. Being very familiar with the bow herself, she knew the sound of a shot about to be taken. Without looking for the source, she leapt to another low wall and ducked. She heard the whish of the bolt failing to find its mark and speeding past her to thunk into a back wall somewhere.

Grandma Prudy's eyes had closed while she relaxed leaned back over the washing sink. Ms. Emma washed her hair and massaged her scalp in an unhurried and fabulously professional manner. Ms. Emma's hands could be considered finely tuned instruments. After decades of practice, she knew exactly what to do, how to move, and exactly how much pressure to exert to give her clients the finest experience possible.

Ms. Emma paused as the CD player on the shelf above her skipped. She shrugged and bent again to her task only to find her customer's eyes open and looking decidedly displeased. Grandma Prudy heard the thunk of the virtual arrow as it slammed into the virtual wall superimposed over the back wall of the beauty parlor. She could clearly see the evil-looking bolt by slightly adjusting her eyes.

"I am so sorry Ms. Emma." Grandma Prudy said evenly. "Could you be a dear and wrap my hair up. I think I need to check on my grandchildren. I am afraid they may be getting into mischief."

Now, Ms. Prudy, you know those grandchildren of yours are the best behaved children for miles around." Ms. Emma chided as she turned off the rinse water and reached for the requested towel.

"Normally, I agree with you but today is their birthday and their spirits are a bit high today." Grandma Prudy explained as Ms. Emma wrapped the towel turban style around the wet hair. "Thank you dear, I will be right back."

Grandma Prudy stood up and looked out into the store. Slightly adjusting her eyes, she could clearly see the virtual world superimposed on the real one. Normally, she would have been very impressed at the effort. The problem of virtual to physical interaction meant that someone could get hurt. She hurried out to where she left her intrepid twin grandchildren.

The entire store had been absorbed into the layout of the game. The danger of the situation hit her immediately. If anything actually struck someone, the energy could transfer. Judging by the mayhem about to engulf the store, she needed to hurry. There they sat, right where she had left them, totally engrossed in their new video games.

"Children, children, children!" Grandma Prudy called as she approached them. "Stop playing those things at once."

Both children looked up obediently at Grandma Prudy's voice. They both wore a look of annoyance. What did she want? They had been good. Then they both saw the energy swirling about them superimposing their game world over the entire store.

"Cool." Jasper spoke for both of them.

"Turn those things off, now!" Grandma Prudy had an unexpected edge to her voice. "Before someone gets hurt.

Both grandchildren punched the power buttons

on their consoles, then stared wide eyed as the strangely intriguing world complete with Gur warriors massed for an attach began to dissipate like steam drifting away from the pot. Without their complete concentration and attention to fuel the all too real illusion, the clear stones had nothing to clarify and amplify.

"Oh children, are the two of you all right?" Grandma Prudy's voice returned to its lovingly stern grandmotherly tone.

"We're ok grandma, what happened?" Emily's eyes relayed her worry about having done something done.

"Emily, Jasper my dears." Grandma Prudy hugged them both. "I'm afraid your mother was right. Please let me have your necklaces for now." Seeing the upset look on their faces, she added, "I'll give them back this afternoon when we get home and after we have a long talk about losing yourself in thought and its power. Right now, I have my hair appointment to finish."

The grandchildren watched as their new birthrights disappeared into the depths of their grandmother's purse. Oddly, they didn't feel like playing their new video games again. Somehow just sitting there sounded good to the both of them, for now.

THE CRYSTAL

Kathleen McCarthy

Why on earth did I do that?

That's what I was wondering as I sat on my bed, staring at the crystal. Fist-sized, flawless and perfectly spherical, it was amazingly beautiful, and it wasn't mine. I'd taken it from my boss's desk several hours ago.

And I had no idea why.

Ordinarily I wouldn't even dream of stealing. I didn't need theft to support Grandad and myself, and I do have morals. But something about that crystal called to me. It...I know this sounds crazy, but it made me pick it up, and put it in my pocket. Then, as soon as I got home, it made me take it out and look at it.

It looked harmless, perfectly innocent. It didn't look like something that was capable of mind control, which was the only explanation I could think of after several hours of thinking. Still, I had stolen it. But why on earth would it want me to?

Something shimmered in the depths of the crystal. Something red.

I squinted at it. "What the…"

Suddenly, Grandad, over in the next room, started making the "arrgh" noises that I'd long since figured out meant "I'm hungry." I sighed, dropped the crystal back in my pocket and went to feed him.

Grandad's real name is Marty Prackle, and he's my paternal grandfather. He's senile, and none of his other descendants were willing to take care of him, so the job fell to me, Alexander Prackle. Since I can't afford a nursing home, Grandad lives with me in my apartment, and Mrs. Fenster next door checks in on him while I'm at work.

I bear Grandad no ill will for cursing me with such a horrendous last name. He's my favorite relative. Before she died, Mom always fought with Dad about money, and my older sisters keep squabbling with each other over who's got the best stuff. Sometimes I feel like I'm from a completely different family. I might as well be…Grandad mostly raised me, before he started wandering mentally.

"Hey, Grandad," I said, on an impulse. "What do you make of this?" I took the crystal out and showed it to him.

He went nuts.

He started yelling incomprehensible words that sounded, oddly enough, like Latin. The crystal started to glow, hot and heavy. I dropped it, scared out of my wits, and yelled. The Fensters next door started banging on the walls, yelling for us to shut up.

I barely registered the racket. A woman came out of the crystal.

The first thought that entered my mind (apart from the whole materializing-out-of-the-crystal thing) was that something was wrong about her. Her narrow, oval face had a faintly inhuman look to it, her ears a gentle point, and her wide green eyes were slanted. She was just slightly too thin, slightly too tall, and that blazing red hair was too…red. Something about her was off.

Of course, this was before she marched up to my grandfather and slapped him across the face.

"How dare you abandon me there!" she screamed. "I have been waiting eight hundred years for you to get off your behind and do something!"

"Hey!" I grabbed her arm. "Don't yell at him, he can't understand you!"

"Actually, I can, Alex," Grandad said, perfectly lucid. "Sorry about the deception, but it was necessary. And, Morgiana, dear…"

"Do not act cute and think you can get away with it," she snapped, twisting away from me. Her mouth was a tight, straight line and her eyes blazed. Literally.

"I was about to apologize. I didn't know where you were, and scrying turned up nothing." Grandad carefully extracted himself from his wheelchair and slumped in my armchair with a sigh and a relieved expression.

"Of course scrying did not work. Morgause is too clever to be caught that way." She turned and paced restlessly. I noticed, as I should have before, that she was wearing a black and purple medieval-style dress with black lace drapes at the sleeves and a black rope belt around it. A silver Celtic knot pendant hung from a black satin cord around her neck. She looked like an escapee from a Renaissance Faire.

Grandad sighed. "So it's Morgause we're dealing with again, is it? I should have known."

"Hang on a sec," I said. "Who are you, what are you doing in my apartment, and what the fuck just happened?"

Grandad raised his eyebrows above the pair of old iron spectacles he wore. "Such language, Alex."

The woman turned to me, clearly impatient with my lack of knowledge. Well, excuse me for breathing. "I am Morgiana, I do not yet know what I am doing in your…apartment…and he summoned me from the crystal. That is what just happened."

The icy scorn in her voice stung me. "Well, excuse me! How was I supposed to know that?" I snapped.

"Children, children. Play nicely." Both of us ignored Grandad.

She raised a single eyebrow in my direction. "How were you…You have done a singularly poor job educating this young man with regards to magic, Merlin."

Grandad shook his head. "Times have changed, my love. Most people no longer believe in magic."

Morgiana snorted. "Poor, silly fools."

"Wait," I broke in. "Did you just call Grandad Merlin?"

"It is my name," Grandad said mildly.

"You're Merlin?"

"Yes, of course he is," Morgiana said, sounding extremely annoyed now. "Who else would he be?"

"I don't believe this," I said, hoping to make my opinion very clear. "My grandfather's Merlin, I suppose you're Morgan le Fay…"

"Morgiana!" she snapped.

"Fine. Morgiana le Fay." I rolled my eyes. "I

don't understand how you got into my apartment, or made my grandfather seem like he's sane, but if you're Morgan le Fay, then I'm King Arthur."

Morgiana whipped around to glare at Grandad, who smiled, indulgently. "Actually, Alex," he said, "you are."

I stared at him, feeling that I'd been hit in the back of the head with a board.

Wait. Maybe I had. Maybe this was all a dream. Maybe I was even now stretched flat out on the floor of my bedroom, while Grandad made his "arrgh" noises from the other room.

"Fool," Morgiana snapped. "You are not dreaming. This is all far too real for my tastes."

"Temper, Morgiana," Grandad said. "Alex, I would appreciate it if you would say something."

"Gahh," I managed, and sat down hard on the couch.

"Good enough; at least you aren't dead of shock. Now, I'm hungry, so let's eat. Food." Grandad snapped his fingers, and a can dropped into his hand. "No, dolt!" he snapped at thin air. "I meant prepared food!"

"Having trouble with your air elemental again?" Morgiana inquired. It was the first polite sentence I'd heard out of her mouth.

"Again nothing," Grandad grumbled. "The infernal thing has been giving me trouble since I first bound it to me. Ah, here we go." A cauldron of soup had dropped onto the floor in front of us. Grandad snapped his fingers again and bowls and spoons floated in from the kitchen.

"Serve yourself, Morgiana," he said, giving her a bowl and a spoon. She filled her bowl, then abandoned it on a table and continued to pace. "Alex…" Grandad turned to look at me. "I realize this is all very difficult for you to accept, but I must ask you to try."

I blinked, several times, and tried to assimilate all the facts that had just been thrown at me. I couldn't.

"Merlin," Morgiana said suddenly, "satisfy my curiosity on something. Are you really his grandfather?"

"Yes, I really am, and no, you needn't worry. Your mother and I settled anything we had between us a good long time ago."

"Oh, I knew that." She stopped pacing for a few swallows of soup. "That was not what I was worried about."

"As for blood connections, his grandmother is long dead and his father and sisters are an extreme disappointment. I had no other children after Thomas." Grandad…Merlin…settled back onto his seat.

A sudden rage built up and pounced on me. "Grandad," I said, sitting up straight, "let's just assume for a moment that I believe all this and it's all true. Really, Grandad, Prackle?"

"What's wrong with Prackle?" Grandad seemed hurt.

"What's wrong with….Grandad, the kids used to call me Prackle the Spackle."

"I must agree with him on this," Morgiana said. I felt my eyebrows shoot up. Was she finally being nice? "You should have picked something magical," she added. Oh. Guess not.

"Oh, but Prackle is magical, my dear," Grandad said, and chuckled. "Magical in the sense that Morgause would never look for Merlin in a man named Marty Prackle. My sense of dignity in the days when she knew me was, I fear, rather extreme."

"There were times when I believed that you existed solely to make the world a more pompous place," Morgiana said, dryly.

"Okay," I said, trying very hard to come to terms with all of this. "I'm not sure that I can believe you. I mean, what proof have you got? Telling me I'm King Arthur…that's all well and good. But how am

I supposed to believe that?"

"You've put your finger solidly on the trouble with magic, Alex." Grandad sighed. "There is no proof. Belief is the most solid part of magic."

"Unless you do this," Morgiana put in, and twisted her hands in a complicated pattern. Shortly afterwards, a ring of lights appeared and bounced around the room, eventually coming to rest in her long red hair. I admired the effect they had on her hair, bringing out golden highlights that I hadn't seen before, then gave myself a mental shake and returned to the problem at hand.

"Faery lights are all well and good, my dear, but they do wreck your credibility on Avalonne," Grandad said reprovingly.

"Well, we are not on Avalonne, are we?" she asked, and gave her hair a shake. The lights bounced some more and formed a circlet over her forehead.

"Better," he said. "First thing, introductions, which I should have gotten to sooner. Morgiana, my dear, this is my grandson Alexander. Alex, my heart-daughter, Morgiana le Fay."

She nodded, coolly, and I returned it. I didn't ask just what a heart-daughter was, because I had the feeling Grandad wouldn't answer.

Grandad sighed again. "Morgiana, my dear, what

happened?"

"I was stupid," she said, and sat down on the couch. "Morgause told me to come to Stonehenge."

"I thought as much. My dear, what possessed you to answer that summons?"

"She said that she would kill Elisabeth," Morgiana mumbled, turning her face away. "I could not ignore that."

"No, I suppose not." Grandad twisted a finger in his beard. "So you went to Stonehenge…"

"And ended up walking into a spell-circle. She recited the trap-spell before I realized I was in danger."

"Ah. So that is how Morgause survived these years. I assume she put controls on your magic so you couldn't break out…"

"Strong controls, yes." Morgiana shook her head. "The only way for me to be freed is if Morgause breaks the crystal. Which she will never do."

"I'm lost," I announced. "What does all this mean?"

"Morgiana is trapped within the crystal by a spell that binds most of her magic," Grandad explained. "The only way to break the spell is to break the crystal. Which reminds me…must it be Morgause?"

"I am not sure. I cannot test the spell very well

from inside it. But if you would have a look at it…" Morgiana got up, stooped gracefully and retrieved the crystal, handing it to Grandad.

He muttered over the crystal for quite some time, peering into it and occasionally uttering a word in Latin or Greek. Eventually he shook his head and looked up. "It must be the caster of the spell. I assume that means Morgause. And it controls much of your magic…"

"But not all." Morgiana touched her circlet of lights.

"I fail to see how faery lights can help us in our present predicament."

Morgiana gave Grandad a level stare. "Alexander," she said, without looking at me, "where did you get the crystal?"

Confused, I answered, "My boss had it. On her desk. I just…something made me take it…"

Grandad and Morgiana exchanged looks, then Grandad said, "Your past…associations with Morgiana, I believe. Her soul would call to yours."

"How?" I asked.

She raised her eyebrow. "I also would like an explanation."

Grandad looked between us, and sighed. "The present is not a particularly auspicious time to rectify this misunderstanding."

A beat, in which Morgiana raised her eyebrow again. "Um, Grandad," I said, "a translation would be nice."

"What? Oh. My apologies. I don't think it would be a good idea to explain now. What's the name of the senator you work for? I always forget."

"Sarah Douglas," I said, still confused. "She's a Republican from Maryland."

Grandad snorted softly. "I never did trust Republicans. Morgiana, my dear…"

"Yes, I am certain that no one but Morgause and Alexander touched the crystal until you yourself did just a minute ago," she said, with the air of one who has been asked the same question once too often.

"Ah. Well, I see no hope for it." Grandad sighed. "You must go back in the crystal, my dear, and Alex…"

"Yeah?" I sat up straighter.

"You have to take the crystal back."

Morgiana and I both objected quite strenuously to this. Finally, Grandad convinced us it was the only way, citing the fact that the crystal (and the spell with it) could only be broken by Morgause. We decided that I would take the crystal back and casually leave it where Morgause could accidentally break it. Once she did, Morgiana's freedom would be assured, and she could confront her half-sister at her own leisure. A crappy plan, I know, but the only thing we could come up with.

Of course, things never go the way they're planned.

I got into the office all right, said hi to my office mate Brian, and sat down to work, trying to hide my nerves. The crystal hung heavy in my pocket, constantly reminding me that an innocent (if somewhat acidic) woman's freedom depended on me, and if I screwed up, she would be trapped for the rest of eternity.

Not a very pleasant feeling.

Add to that the equally unpleasant feeling that if I failed, I would never see Morgiana again. I'd grown to at least respect her during that one night while she and Grandad and I talked, and I could see that Grandad had a real affection for her. If I screwed up...well, I wouldn't think about that now.

Sarah Douglas came in promptly at nine, and greeted us all with a cheery wave as she sailed into her office. She looked a bit frazzled this morning, but otherwise normal. She certainly didn't look like a sorceress who's just lost her main power source. I found myself having doubts all over again. How could my scatterbrained, dedicated and slightly flirty boss be Morgause de Arevail, the evil sorceress Morgiana and Grandad had described?

At nine-thirty, Kate, our office manager, came out into the main office and called my name. "Yeah?" I said, trying to look as if I'd been working instead of worrying about the plan and my part in it.

"Boss wants to see you, Alex," she said, coming over to my desk. "But don't worry, it didn't sound like anything too serious."

"Yeah, all right." I pretended to close some applications and got up. "Maybe she wants to give me a raise." Kate and I had a good laugh about that, then I went over to Sarah's office, pretending to be casual. In reality, a sick feeling thudded into my stomach. Did she know…?

"Alex!" Sarah said, warmly, as I walked in. "Listen, I'm glad I caught you. I lost a paperweight the other day. You might have seen it…a round crystal?"

"Yeah, I saw it," I said, as casually as I could. "You're telling me that thing was a paperweight? Round stuff doesn't usually work very well for that."

Sarah laughed. "A gag gift from my sister. You're right, it doesn't work very well, but I love her and I thought I might as well use it."

I swear, I could hear Morgiana grinding her teeth.

"But you haven't seen it since then," she continued.

"Nope!" Cheerful lie. Now where in her office could I...

"All right, enough," Sarah said, in a completely different tone. Cold as ice, hard as steel. I know, cliché, but appropriate.

Okay, so she's on to us. What do I do now?

I'd asked Grandad that very same question last night, and memorized his answer: when in doubt, lie like a rug.

"E-enough what?" I asked, trying to sound innocent. The stutter didn't help.

She sneered at me. Yes, sneered. "Enough of this pretense, Arthur. I know they told you everything. Where is the crystal?"

"Sarah, I really have no idea what you're talking about." I began to edge towards the door.

Sarah raised a hand and twisted it. The door locked behind me. Shit.

"Where is the crystal?" she asked again.

Fine. Be that way. Now how do I save Morgiana?

And then it hit me. Staff baseball game, two months ago. Sarah playing catcher and dropping even the easiest of throws… "Fine," I said, standing up straighter and acting like I wasn't afraid of her. "You want it? Here. Catch." I pulled the crystal out of my pocket and pitched her my best fastball.

She caught it easily.

Too late, I remembered that magic, especially that of a sorceress powerful enough to control Morgiana le Fay, can do just about anything. "Oh, shit."

Sarah laughed, a much uglier sound then her earlier carefree giggles. "You, Arthur, are in some trouble."

"I would say so, yes," I said, edging towards the door again. Maybe I could yell for help?

"I have soundproofed the office," Sarah said, as if reading my mind. Shit, maybe she really could read my mind. In which case I was screwed.

"Oh? Good for you. What are you going to do now?"

"As if I'd tell you." She prowled around the desk towards me. "All you need to know is that it involves you and pain. And quite possibly my dear sister here." She caressed the smooth surface of the crystal almost lovingly.

"Half-sister," I corrected. "She did tell me that much."

"Tsk, tsk." Sarah tapped the crystal. "Morgiana

has always had much too big a mouth. And much too soft a spot for mere humans."

Okay. That was out of the blue. I raised my eyebrows. "Excuse me? Last I heard you were human too."

"I have some faery blood," Sarah snapped. Ouch. Struck a nerve, did I? Maybe I can play on this…

"Do you really? I think you're just a silly little witch playing with powers you can't understand," I said, forcing a smile onto my face. I hoped she would take the falseness of that smile for smugness. "Morgiana is ten times more powerful than you will ever be."

Sarah hissed with anger. "Is that so? Well, I control her now, don't I? So I am more powerful than her!"

Uh-oh. Shaky ground.

"Not from what I heard from her. Trap spells are the easiest of all magic, am I right?"

A wild guess, but apparently a correct one. Sarah's face contorted with rage. "I'll show you how powerful I am!" she snarled, and threw the first thing that came to hand.

Which was the crystal.

It flew towards me, gaining unnatural speed as it went, and no doubt would have cracked my skull if it had actually made contact. But thanks to the incessant bullying of my younger days (which, in turn, was thanks to Grandad's whimsical sense of what made a good last name) I had very good reflexes.

I ducked right and the crystal shattered against the wall.

Sarah shrieked, a world of loss and hatred in that sound. The falling pieces of crystal showered around a rapidly-growing figure.

Morgiana didn't even look at me, only gazed at her half-sister with anger in her narrowed eyes. "Morgause," she said, evenly. "It has been a very long time since we last faced as equals."

"It has," Sarah said, retreating behind her desk. Hatred burned in her eyes. "But then you were never equal to me, halfbreed."

Morgiana didn't even blink. "I would have thought you had risen above petty insults by now." She sounded almost regretful.

"Petty insults?" Sarah made that ugly sound that passed for a laugh again. "Petty insults, you call it. I don't think so, Morgiana."

"Whatever you have to say, say it," Morgiana said. "I have much to do, not least of which is to make sure you cannot harm me or mine ever again."

"How would you do that? Kill me? You don't have the guts and you know it."

"Do not push me, Morgause." Deadly anger grew in Morgiana's voice.

"Don't push me, don't push me!" Sarah mocked, and started to laugh. I couldn't help but think that this was a particularly stupid, not to mention immature, thing to do. Sarah seemed to be reverting to a three-year-old in front of my eyes.

Morgiana sighed. "Have you anything productive to say?"

Sarah just kept laughing. Yeah, I didn't think so either.

"Cover your eyes, Alexander," Morgiana said, quietly.

I did as I was told. A bright flash devoured the room, and when I opened my eyes, I was lying flat on my back, a cut across my forehead, dazed and disoriented. The others in the office crowded around me, anxious faces filling my vision. There was no sign of either Morgiana or Sarah.

"No, officer, I don't know what happened. Yes, officer, I was talking to my boss when it happened. No, officer, I didn't hear anything, and can I please go home now because I'm tired of being interrogated, goddamnit!"

Grandad raised his eyebrows. "Really, Alex. You said that to a policeman?"

I sighed. "No, I didn't. I'm not that stupid. What happened?"

"Damned if I know. Morgiana probably pulled some kind of kamikaze move." He sounded entirely too calm for this extraordinary and slightly painful announcement.

I jerked upright and stared at him. "You're kidding. You've got to be kidding."

"No, unfortunately, I am not." He sounded regretful, now. "I do not know if she thought she could defeat Morgause or not…but I tell you this, Alex. Morgiana is a far better sorceress then she allows herself to believe. She protected you, she defeated Morgause. Whether she herself survived…well, we can only hope."

"Really, Alex, are you bringing home work again?"

I sighed and resisted the urge to throw something at my grandfather. Three months since he'd regained his supposedly lost sanity, and he was acting like he'd never been faking it. His doctors were completely mystified, something I suspected he got a big kick out of. "No, I'm not. Not as if it mattered. I don't have a social life and I'm not likely to have one. As you well know."

He rolled his eyes and buried his nose in his newspaper again. "You need to get out more. Oh, look, this should be interesting, an exhibition at the Athenaeum gallery. That's just down the street."

"Art?" I made a face. "Don't try to inject culture into me. It didn't work when I was fifteen, it won't work now."

"Yes, well. I think this particular exhibition will interest you. Anna Lefay—a very lovely artist, by the by—specializes in fantasy art."

"Dirty old man," I said, meaning the 'lovely artist' comment. "Don't try to fix me up either."

"Wouldn't dream of it," Grandad said, sounding entirely too cheerful. "Come on, we can go now."

I rolled my eyes but allowed him to grab my arm and propel me out the door, down the street and into the Athenaeum.

To give my grandfather credit, the exhibition was quite good. Many of the paintings were illustrations from Arthurian legends, and I wondered if this was a coincidence. One in particular intrigued me; a portrait of a young, red-haired woman, done in loving detail, and entitled, simply, "Elaine."

"She reminds me of Morgiana," I said, gesturing at the portrait.

"Yes, she does, doesn't she?" Grandad seemed quite happy that I'd made the connection. "Let's see, our artist should be coming any moment now."

"What did I say about…" My voice died.

"Hello, Alexander, Merlin," Morgiana said, coming up to us. "I am sorry for the deception, but I needed to see if I could survive on my own."

"Which you have, quite handily. You are far more intelligent then you give yourself credit for, my dear." Grandad glanced at me, and added, crossly, "Don't just stand there with your mouth hanging open, boy! Say something!"

"I…you're alive?" I managed.

She smiled, very slightly. "Yes, I am. Thank you for your concern."

"Concern!" I exploded. "Jesus, Morgiana, it's been nearly three months! I thought you were dead!" Her smile faltered, but before she could say anything, Grandad coughed, bringing my attention to him. "And you! You knew about this, didn't you? Is the entire world in a conspiracy to keep me in the dark?"

"I'm sure Agent Mulder would agree with you," Grandad observed, dryly. He'd gotten obsessed with a variety of TV shows while exercising his newfound sanity, the X-Files not least. "However, conspiracies are not the topic under discussion here. I assure you, Alex, I did not know that Morgiana was still alive or I would have told you. I did, however, meet her today at this exhibition. I thought showing was better then telling in this case."

"And he was quite prompt about it," Morgiana added. "For him."

I sighed, defeated. "Fine. Just…don't do it again."

"I won't," she assured me.

"Anyway, I love your artwork," I said. "Who's the dude with the shiny gold armor? It looks like he's going to get it scuffed."

For the first time since I had known her, Morgiana laughed.

A Fool And His Honey

Nick Aires

You're a fool, Henry. You're nothing but a screw-up, Henry. I don't know why I ever married you, Henry.

"I'll show her who the fool is," Henry grumbled as he walked into the woods behind his house. Their house was pretty much the only thing they still owned anymore. Henry had lost almost everything gambling. Now, he and his wife were practically starving to death. His lazy, nagging wife felt it necessary to remind him that their predicament was entirely his fault every waking moment of the day.

But Henry had a plan, not that any of his last dozen plans had worked, but this one surely would! There was a giant beehive Henry had spotted in one of the trees out back, and Henry was going to sell the honey it surely contained.

Henry'd had the foresight to bring a bucket for the honey, but he'd not thought to bring anything else. So, when he got to the beehive, he simply stuck his hand into it.

Suddenly, an enraged bee burst out of a hole in the hive.

"You wouldn't be planning on stealing my honey now, would you?" asked the bee with false sweetness.

Henry froze, astonished, "I...I...I..." he spluttered.

Quickly recovering from his initial surprise, Henry stood his ground. "My wife and I are very hungry. So yes, I am planning on taking this honey, and no little bug is going to stand in my way!"

Realizing that the big, burly man probably wasn't afraid of being stung, the bee tried a different tactic. "Well, I'm a magical bee, so how about I grant you and your wife three wishes in exchange for your leaving my hive alone?"

Henry guffawed. "Yeah, right — like I'm going to believe that you have magical powers!"

"You have no problem with the fact that a bee is talking to you, but it's too much of a stretch to believe that I can also grant wishes?" the bee asked derisively.

"Heh, you got me there," Henry replied, scratching his head. "All right, fine. Three wishes instead of honey. But if you're lying, I'll be back later to steal your honey and smash your hive to bits. You got that?"

The bee merely smiled.

Henry raced back to the house to share the good news with his wife.

He found her sitting on the couch, draining a bottle of beer. It was a home brew, but it was better than nothing. In fact, each one seemed to taste better to Lorraine, this current one being her seventh.

Henry was tired of seeing her wasted, but he was too wound up to let it bring him down.

Seeing the silly grin on Henry's face, Lorraine inquired as to what imbecilic thing he'd done this time.

For a moment Henry considered not telling her, but he was too excited not to talk about it. He gave her an animated account of his encounter with the magical bee.

Lorraine laughed so hard at her husband's tall tale, that she snorted beer threw her nose. "You know what I wish for," she cackled, drunkenly slurring her words. "I wish I had some chips and hotdogs to go with this beer…"

"NOOOOOO!" Henry screamed, but sadly too late. Suddenly, out of the air appeared the hotdogs and potato chips she'd carelessly wished for.

"What have you done?" Henry wailed. "Of all the stupid, dim-witted, idiotic things to wish for! All the times you've called me a fool, you're the fool! I wish you were a hotdog!"

No sooner had the words left his mouth when there materialized an enormous wiener, cooked to perfection, lying on the couch.

Henry was mortified. He'd just repeated his wife's foolish mistake.

With just one wish left, there seemed only one thing he could do.

"I wish for a six-foot long hotdog bun!"

As Henry fruitlessly searched his empty refrigerator for mustard and relish, something in the back of his mind bothered him, something about his last wish. Did he make a mistake?

Henry was too hungry to think about the wish any longer. But as he was about to take a bite of the jumbo dog, it came to him: "Oh no! What have I done? I should have wished for condiments too!"

BLACK MARY

James Ferris

The autumn Memphis air awash with the sweet smell of cotton candy swirled around children squealing in glee as they ran from booth to booth. The dark of night found itself held at bay by the flashing lights of the rides and the colored floods that defined the temporary carnival grounds. Parents acted as bearers for stuffed animals, half eaten hotdogs, and cups of lemonade. Music crackled and blared from aged speakers as barkers vied with each other for the people's attention and money.

Rides whirled out into the night sky giving the thrill of danger but safely returning their passengers to the earth. Some looked grateful to be back on the ground, others looked forward in anticipation to the adrenaline rush of the next ride. Two of the young men in the crowd carried an entirely different look in their eyes as they walked between the rides and trailers. Alex "Rat" Johnson and Lester "Ape" Apfel stopped in a semi-dark spot where there were few people.

"Dude, I am telling you. Look around you. They've been here all week doing nothing but taking in cash," Rat said with as much emphasis as he could without shouting. His narrow face looked hard beyond his years. He pulled out his cigarettes and lit one. Ape caught the pack as Rat tossed it to him. He lit his own and stood there smoking for a minute while he thought.

"So when do you think they should get hit?" Ape finally asked. He took a deep drag and waited.

"I figure they're pulling out tomorrow night, so tonight looks good to me." Rat answered.

"Ok smart guy, where do they have all this money stashed?"

"Let's do a little more checking around and see what looks good." Rat dropped his butt to the ground and crushed it out under his heel. Ape followed suit as they walked back out into the strobbing and swirling lights. They hung out by the vendors at the rides and acted interested in the customers that were being entertained. Each booth had one person who took the tickets and stuffed them into a plain wooden box with a hole in the lid and a padlock.

They wandered by the ticket booth and bought a few dollars worth. They paid careful attention to the armed guard sitting almost out of view in the back of the booth behind a poorly drawn curtain. Old and more than half asleep, he would not be a serious threat to their nefarious plans. Ape tapped Rat on the shoulder and pointed out a couple of carnies quietly walking back and forth from the rear of the freak show to the booths. They were exchanging empty boxes for the full ones. Ape and Rat found a food booth near the center of the carnival where they could sit without attracting unwanted attention. They bought a couple of drinks and corndogs. Slowly they ate and carefully they watched.

"They're pretty smart." Ape said quietly as he leaned towards Rat. "I would've never thought to hit the freak show."

"That's why we sit and we watch." Rat replied as he took another bite.

"What do you want to do next?"

Rat leaned back and looked around then leaned back in to his partner. "I want to check out that freak show."

"Good idea." Ape stood up with those words and waited for Rat. Together, they wandered aimlessly towards the entrance to the exhibit.

The sign read "Black Mary's Voodoo Oddities". The music, suitably weird and "voodoo" sounding, haunted the entrance. The garishly painted signs promised oddities of all types including a tattooed lady, a snake charmer, and a fortuneteller. They gave the middle-aged woman mindlessly tending the booth their tickets. Ape smiled at her while he turned slightly to fit the massive bulk of his upper body though the narrow entryway. She smiled back missing a front tooth. The layout of the exhibit was simple; walk through the darkness towards the lit booths to see the attractions.

"Damn baby, how long you been getting stuck with the ink?" Rat half exclaimed and half asked as he stepped up and saw the tattooed woman. The slender woman dressed only in a very thin bikini sitting on a tall stool turned slowly. Nearly every inch of her body glowed in magnificent multicolored artwork. As she curved towards Rat, he could see that even her face was covered.

She smiled at the question she answered hundreds of times a day. "I've been tattooing for about ten years now."

"Lady, I got a couple of tattoos but damn!" Rat was amazed. Ape just looked politely from behind his friend. He didn't like needles so the tattoos made him a little uncomfortable. Rat continued to stare at her. "I bet getting your face done hurt."

"It doesn't hurt long." She smiled with the same professional smile she had been using for years. She contortioned slowly on the stool so the young men could see that she was indeed covered completely.

The thought of all those needles finally overcame Ape. He stepped to the next booth. This one claimed to feature some kind of giant rat. Not impressed, Ape just shook his head. He had seen something just like it on TV. He kept moving further into the darkness of the tent.

The snake charmer turned out to be another attractive young woman with a boa constrictor. The snake, sufficiently large and she sufficiently barely dressed, held his attention until Rat caught up to him. The reptile slowly wound itself in and around her ample charms. Rat flicked his tongue out snake-like at them. Both the woman and the snake wore the same unseeing gaze in their eyes. The young men moved on.

Booth after booth of things that might have been amazing thirty years ago filled the tent. Spiders and scorpions could be bought at pet stores now. Piranhas are even common in aquariums these days. Rat and Ape looked in each booth. The displays did not interest them. Remembering where things were located so they didn't stumble over them later held their true fascination.

The end of the exhibit neared when they saw the star attraction. The sign said the display held for their viewing pleasure a lizard-man from the mysterious Amazonian rainforest. Ape and Rat, both fascinated and repulsed by the wretched creature in the display, could not help but stare intently. It resembled some kind of huge lizard. The limbs, oddly too long for its size, sat motionless. The end of the front legs possessed a pair of what appeared to be clawed hands.

Its head proved to be the worst part of the wretched apparition. The top of it appeared swollen or rounded, not flat like a lizard's head is supposed to be. The eyes, big and brown like a human's, stared forward with the same unseeing gaze as the rest of the exhibits. It's fat pink tongue flicked out every so often. They just kept staring at it. Rat tapped on the glass. It hissed and shook its head as if disgusted with its audience.

"Man, did you see that? That's just gross." Ape couldn't be quiet any longer.

"Dude, that is one sick looking lizard," Rat stated in agreement with Ape. They watched as it painfully pulled its bulk around until its back provided their only view of the beast. "Well, that thing is in the right place. That thing is a freak! Come on, man. I've seen enough."

"But have you seen your future?"

The disembodied and heavily accented voice nearly shook them off of their bones. Both of them jumped back ready to fight or run.

"What the fu…." Rat began before the voice interrupted him.

"Sorry, I didn't mean to scare you. I thought you saw me sitting here."

Ape and Rat looked towards the voice and could just barely make out the silhouette of a heavy woman sitting behind a table. Wrapped in the shadows, she could see the customers long before they could her. They felt as well as saw her lean forward. A slight rustling sound preceded the abrupt appearance of a flame. She lit the candle in the center of the table. The lighter disappeared into the folds of her sleeves. The flickering candle revealed the brightly colored robes and headdress of the fortuneteller. The whites of her eyes nearly glowed against her luxuriantly ebony skin. Her teeth showed through her knowing smile and reflected the eerie yellow radiance of the single candle.

"Would you like me to tell you your fortune?" The fortuneteller asked again with that heavy Caribbean accent. She spread her hand out palms up on the table as she spoke.

"I don't need anyone to tell me my future." Rat declined as he stepped past her booth. "You damn near scared me to death."

Ape looked at her for a long uncomfortable moment then just shook his head from side to side. He turned to follow Rat.

"I'll give you both a little free advice then." The fortuneteller called softly after them. "You're coming to a crossroads that will decide the rest of your lives. Choose very carefully."

"Yeah, whatever, thanks, see ya." Rat called back to her then to Ape he said, "Let's go man. I've seen enough."

Ape quietly followed his partner out of the exhibit and back into the bright lights of the carnival. Plans had to be made. As they walked away, Ape felt a cold shiver run down his spine.

Just after three in the morning, the carnival noise had transformed to complete quiet, the music off and the flashing lights out. The grounds, nothing more than a bizarre collection of twisted shadows in the deepest part of the night, stood in silent anticipation of the return of the dawn a few short hours away. Even the moon had left the sky. Ape and Rat walked quietly towards their goal. They did not speak. Only well-practiced hand signals stolen from military movies were exchanged between them. Perfectly on cue, they split up and walked completely around the exhibit. Not a living soul could be seen or heard. The area supplied perfect cover for them. As they met on the far side, they walked up to each other and made a few gestures. They both nodded in comprehension then walked to the back of the exhibit tent. Rat pulled an evil-looking knife from its sheath strapped to his ankle and cut along the ground at the edge of the material. Ape stood watch. Nothing stirred, not even the fall breeze. Hearing the click of the knife back into its sheath, Ape reached down and lifted the edge of the material creating a space for Rat to wriggle through. Once Rat had disappeared into the blackness of the tent, Ape lay down and crawled through the gap Rat now held for him.

They looked around in the interior dimness. They had entered through the back of one of the booths. Now empty, its contents stored away for the night. They moved carefully without any light to the front of the booth. Rat stepped over the low barrier and out onto the walkway first. Ape followed quietly. Every few steps, Ape would tap Rat on the shoulder and they would stop and listen. Nothing but the quiet of the middle of the night reached their ears. Nothing in the darkness impeded their progress. A couple of more booths and they would reach the booth where the fortuneteller sat. They figured that the door leading to the business office had to be hidden in the back of that booth.

Behind the black curtains covering the wall, the door was discovered by sense of touch. Their hands sweaty with excitement left faint trails, invisible in the gloom, as they traced the wood until the knob could be located. Rat had the lock open in a few moments. Ape clicked on a cloth muffled flashlight. The interior of the office witness paid mute homage to their disreputable skill.

They looked around briefly. Everything in the office had to be portable thus providing few hiding places. They began quietly searching all the obvious places. Ape quickly found the only locked file cabinet in the trailer. He pulled a jagged looking bastard file from his own ankle sheath and in less than a minute sawed through the restraining bolt. In the back of the bottom drawer, there lay their prize, a canvas bank deposit bag filled with stacks of wrapped bills. Experience told him that tonight's haul would be in the thousands not their normal hundreds. He patted Rat on the shoulder with his free hand as he happily handed him the bag. Rat undid his belt and strapped the bag to his body with it. Unhurriedly, they returned the office to its original state before their search. This would help slow the discovery of the theft. They made one final check. Everything looked good. Ape put away the flashlight as they reentered the exhibit area.

They only had a few more steps to take until freedom through their slit in the tent wall when they heard something move. They both froze. The sound touched them again in the blackness. Rat slowly reached for the knife at his ankle. Ape flexed his huge arms. The talent of being good at breaking into places meant nothing unless it coupled with the ability to get out, no matter what or who was in the way. They waited a few more moments. Just as Rat took his next step towards escape, the horrible scrapping sound issued forth again. It was close.

"Kill me."

The barely recognizable words hissed out of the blackness. Their eyes barely had time to find the source of the tortured plea before the shape leapt from the floor towards them. Rat and Ape both fell back in fright. The scramble made too much noise for vocal silence to be of any value anymore. They could see the shape coming at them again.

"For God's sake, kill me."

Rat scrambled out of the way hissing through his teeth, "Ape, grab it and shut it up."

Ape obeyed and jumped onto the back of the dark shape. The leathery skin, covered in scales, slid under his hands. He fought hard to gain control; fighting both the dark shape and his natural mammalian urge to flee anything reptilian. Ape rolled the thing across the ground until he could get a steady grip on it. His hands found what felt like the limbs. With a massive effort, he managed to twist the limbs over into a locking arm bar. Pressing down with the weight of his chest, he could just hold his unknown scaly adversary long enough grab the flashlight and roll it out onto the floor towards Rat.

"Rat, grab the light. What the hell is this thing?" Ape said through his teeth trying not to let his voice carry.

Rat snatched up the light, flicked it on, and pointed it back at his partner and their attacker. The too-human eyes of the giant lizard-man blinked in the glare. Ape had a beefy arm around its neck and the other around its body. He stood up hauling the heavy creature with him.

"Have pity. Kill me." It barely managed to hiss

from those reptilian lips.

"Oh damn. That thing can talk!" Rat cried out in horror. The display lights in the tent came on before he could say anything else.

"I told you boys to choose carefully." The fortuneteller said from the office door. All three of them spun to face her. Still wearing her colored robes, she looked like she had been waiting for them.

"You, the one called Ape, put him down very carefully. He's worth a lot to me," she pointed as she spoke. He carefully set the giant reptile down on the ground and stood back up.

"She's called Black Mary because she does black magic." The reptile hissed as it lay there.

"That's enough out of you. You get back to your bed and leave them be." Mary scolded. She made shooing gestures with her hands as the wretched creature began to drag its self down the walkway.

Ape and Rat suddenly realized why it had asked them to kill it. They looked at each other then at Mary. The amount of danger they now faced began to creep into their souls. True terror began to etch itself onto their faces. Mary didn't look scared. She looked annoyed.

"That's right. Poor old Reggie, he slithered in here one night to do some stealing. I just make sure he earns an honest living these days." Mary looked hard into their eyes. "Now, you two come in here and try to take our money. I warned you both you had a crossroads coming. You could've chosen to go home tonight and sleep in your beds. Instead, you chose to come down here and try to rob us. So boys, what should I do with you?"

Rat slowly pulled the bag out from under his belt. He tossed it under hand to her feet.

"Listen lady, you got your money back. We're just gunna leave they way we came in. No harm, no foul." Rat tried to keep his voice from cracking in fear as he spoke. The thought that the pathetic creature had been a man overwhelmed his mind. Part of him did not believe it and part of him screamed for him to run for his life. Sweat built up on Ape's brow. He had no choice but to wait for Rat to make a move.

"It's not that easy, what did he call you? Oh yes, Rat." Black Mary began to explain. "We travel from river town to river town. Anywhere the old river does its magic. No matter if is New Orleans, Vicksburg, or Memphis. We set up our tents. We do our shows. We give the good folks a good time. We do no one any harm. I don't mess with those who leave me alone. Those who don't, become my best exhibits. So boys, what do you want to be?"

Black Mary stepped forward, over the bag of money. She held up her hands and let her sleeves fall out of the way. The lights began to flicker and dim. Black Mary's eyes turned black as pitch. The young men panicked. Rat, with knife in hand, ran for the tent wall. Ape grabbed the front of the closest booth and flung it at Mary. It never touched her. She just raised her hands higher and mumbled a few words. She clapped her hands together and cold blue lightning arced out across the room. Sparks flew from wherever the deadly power touched. One bolt caught Rat just as he plunged the knife into the material of the wall. He twisted and danced in the blue surges of energy like a broken marionette. Ape ran pulling down everything he could behind him. Everywhere he turned, the unearthly energy arced in front of him. Finally, the energy found its target, right over his heart.

When Black Mary dropped her hands, the unearthly energy stopped and her victims fell heavily to the ground. She strolled down the littered walkway to Rat's final resting place then over to Apes.

"Hmmm, I think I will have a couple of new signs made in the morning. The Rat Boy – Half Man, Half Rat, found in the old city sewers of Atlanta.

Yes that will do." Black Mary smiled as she thought out loud. "The Missing Link – From the Darkest Africa. How does that sound to you boys? Are you ready to earn an honest living for old Black Mary?"

HEIRLOOMS

Albert Coelho

"John, John, wake up."

"What?" John whispered, staring at the ring that had just fallen from his hand.

Tom was grabbing John by the shoulders. "John, what's wrong with you?"

"What's going on? Where am I?" John mumbled, still dazed.

"John, you're in the antique shop."

"I was having this dream…"

"What dream? You were just picking up that antique ring when suddenly your face went blank. You're as white as a ghost. What happened to you?"

"I don't want to talk about it, Fill me in on what's happening."

"What do you mean, fill you in?

"I can't seem to remember anything but that hallucination."

"You were blanked out for about a minute until you dropped the ring, that's all."

"Tom, please tell me what we're doing here," John said, bewildered.

"We are investigating the kidnapper," Tom answered, his brow wrinkling.

"What kidnapper?" John said, his puzzled expression still narrowing his eyes.

"Jesus! What's happened to you? Don't you remember?" Tom was raising his voice.

"Damn it Tom, I just told you I don't remember! Please fill me in from the beginning." John snapped loudly.

"OK. We got this case," Tom sighed, "about the kid, your distant relative, that was kidnapped fifteen years ago?" He searched John's face for recognition. "His father didn't pay until the kidnappers cut the kids ear off? He paid? They found the kid."

"Yeah, right. The kid thought he saw the kidnapper's ring here in our uncle's Antique shop, so he came to us to investigate." John smiled.

"Right!" Tom said, relieved.

"And we came into this antique shop to check out the ring the kid saw in here."

"Right, but when you picked up the ring, you went into this kinda trance," Tom said, waving his hands and wobbling his head.

"The ring, where is it?"

"You dropped it. It's here on the counter." Tom said, reaching for the ring.

"Don't touch it!" John grabbed his hand.

"Take it easy, man," Tom was puzzled.

"You don't understand, the second I touched that ring, I felt like I was sucked into a tube of light and I ended up in the past. Iwent to this place, like I was this Lord Vahn guy…"

"My Lord, My Lord!" the servant shouted..

"What… what is it?" Lord Vahn broke from his daze.

"My Lord, you were in some kind of evil trance."

"What do you mean?" He shook his head.

"When you picked up the magician's ring, you went into a trance. You were in that trance until you dropped the ring." Lord Vahn's eyes opened wide.

"Where is it now?"

"There, at your feet," the servant bent to retrieve the ring.

"Do not touch it! Give me your dagger; I will pick it up with that, if you see me going into trance again knock it from my hand."

Picking up the ring with the dagger, Lord Vahn placed it into a plate on the table. He looked at it suspiciously.

"What news?" he asked the servant.

"The magician has been captured; He is being brought here now."

"Good." He snapped. "Get me wine and let me rest until he arrives. Bring him to the dungeon and chain him to the wall before you summon me." Lord Vahn sat down heavily, resting his head in his hands.

"Yes Lord" Albrecht said, bowing and stepping backwards. …

"Put that ring into the box. Use the pencil to pick it up."

"OK, John." Tom slid the pencil through the ring and lifted it into the box, as if it were a scorpion or something. He shivered as it dropped.

"Uncle Pete, where did you get this ring?" The detective questioned the shop owner.

"Listen Johnny, I don't want any trouble." The shop keeper said, holding his hands up.

"No trouble, Uncle Pete. Just, please, tell me where you got this ring."

"It goes with that Sword that's broken in half." He motioned to the box on the display shelf. "They are heirlooms, been in our family for hundreds of years, I guess."

"But how did Bobby recognize this ring as belonging to one of the kidnappers?"

"Beats me, Johnny," Uncle Pete, looked honestly confused.

"This has never been out of your sight?"

"Actually, I have had it locked up in the box with the sword. I never took it out until last week, when I decided to try to sell it."

"Did you touch it?" John queried.

"I picked them up with a polishing cloth. I don't think I ever actually touched them with my bare hands." Uncle Pete said, squinting, as if trying to remember.

"Let me see the sword." John nodded toward the box.

The antique dealer held the box out and John picked up the sword…

"Captain, Captain Van." The Commander softly shook his captain's shoulder.

"Yes, what is it Tom?" The captain asked, shaking his head.

"Are you OK?"

"Yeah, why?" He looked stunned.

"You are as white as a ghost. You seemed to have blacked out for a while when you touched that old sword from earth."

"Yeah, I decided to look through these family heirlooms I just dug up from the chest I inherited last year. When I reached for the sword, I went into this dream like trance. For a while I thought I was this Private Investigator looking into some kidnapping back in the twentieth century.

"Wow, really? And here you are in the middle of your own kidnapping case. Weird."

"What have you found Tom?"

"They have made a DNA match. The ear is your son's."

"Damn it! What do they want?" the captain rose from his chair and stepped toward the monitor at the back wall.

"I don't know Sir." The Commander shrugged.

"That sword I just dropped, pick it up with your something and place it back into the box, please. Don't touch it."

"Yes Sir. If you don't mind my asking, where did that sword come from?" He asked, as he stooped to pick up the sword with his notebook, sliding the cover under it and sandwiching it into his papers.

"An heirloom from earth. It's been in my family for thousands of years, I guess." The captain said, standing in front of the console with his hands clasped behind his back.

"That ring too?" He pointed to the ring lying in the box on the table

The captain reached for it. "Yes this ring…"

"John, you went out again." Tom was shaking John by the shoulders.

"Yeah," John said a bit dazed but suspecting a connection between his blackouts and the heirlooms, "put this sword away, just like the ring, don't touch it."

"OK." Tom gingerly took the sword with his handkerchief.

"Uncle Pete," John said, turning to the antique dealer, "your cousin's son, Bill swears he saw this ring on the pinky finger of his kidnapper. Is it possible there are two rings?"

"Anything's possible, but I doubt it. I was in Europe collecting valuable Antiques from my family's remains, which were finally released by the German government. My family was almost wiped out in the holocaust. "

"Why do you say you doubt there could be two rings alike?" John asked.

"That ring is made from a metal that I can't identify."

"What?"

"Yeah, it's spooky, it looks like gold, but it doesn't react like it."

"Meaning?"

"It does not bend or melt like ordinary gold. It can't be molded or changed."

"Strange. So you would say this is the only ring of its kind?"

"Probably."

"Did you ever here the name, Mardak?"

"No, I don't think so; I'd remember that I think. Wait a minute, there was this antique dealer my father knew when I was just a kid, his name sounded something like that. Why?" He tilted his head, looking at the detective.

"Where was this and when?"

"We lived three blocks down, on Madison. This old guy used to come by my house once in a while. I don't know anything else about him. Why do you ask?"

"That's the name your nephew told us he remembered the kidnapper using on the phone when he thought the kid wasn't listening. I need to get a closer look at this ring." John took the pencil and lifted the ring to look at it. "Can I use your Jewelers glass?"

"Sure."

As he reached for the glass, the ring slid down the pencil…

"My Lord." The servant said as he entered the

torch-lit room.

"Yes." Lord Vahn roused. He was standing behind his chair staring at the lighted torch.

"He is here." The servant stated coldly.

"I shall come down." Lord Vahn sighed, leaning on the back of his chair.

"My lord, before you go you should know, he has around his neck a dried ear, seeming to be the other ear to match the one he sent."

"My son's other ear!" The Lord started.

"It seems so." The servant said, lowering his head.

"Damn that wizard! I will kill him slowly, once I get my son." The Lord gripped the chair. He was shaking. He swung the chair around and stormed from the room, the servant following.

The quickly descended the stairs toward the dungeon. The servant carried the torch. Lord Vahn seemed not to notice the darkness. As they entered the dungeon, the wizard smiled.

"Where is my son?" The Lord hissed, peering into the magician's eyes.

The magician began laughing. Louder and louder, he laughed.

The rage and fear for his son grew in the Lord.

The magician licked his lips. His teeth had

been filed to razor sharpness. Seeing this, the Lord knew.

With his rage and fear he drew his sword and crashed it into and through the heart of the magician. It went into the wall and broke in half. The magician disappeared. A faint laughter resounded. Mardak was gone, but his ring lay there at Lord Vahn's feet.

Lord Vahn moved back. Angry fear swelled through him. Swooning, he fell to the floor, blood boiling through his brain. The pain from the back of his head screeched through his ears and blackened his vision. He was, no more....

John dropped the ring. He looked around once again bewildered. His hand went to the sword...

"Captain, The patrol has come in. They caught this guy named Mardak, with three golden ears on a chain around his neck. One of them looks like it could be the match to your son's."

The captain was standing by his chair at the communications console.

"What?" The captain's face blanched. He sank heavily into his chair. "Where is he?" he asked in a whisper.

"He tried to escape, but they fired. He vaporized, exploded into thin air."

"What?" He turned quickly to face the Commander.

"He is gone." Tom said.

"But my son," The captain pleaded.

"From the looks of this guy, anything could have happened." The Commander said, shaking his head slowly.

"Show me the interrogation holos of him!" The captain growled, his fear giving in to his anger.

"Yes Sir, here is the video of his entrance onto the station with the patrol." The lieutenant entered something on the console.

Watching the video, the captain could see the man's face. As he watched he saw Mardak glance directly at the camera and laugh. He saw the man's sharpened teeth and he knew what had happened to his son. He opened the box and picked up the Sword…

"Johnny." Tom knocked the sword from the detective's hand and John slowly came to himself again.

After a few moments, John asked his uncle, "This guy, Mardak, that your father knew, did you ever see him close up?"

"Yeah I did once, he was strange. He had these funny looking teeth. They were all like dog's teeth, ya know, sharp I mean."

"Yeah, I think I know what you mean. Let's go Tom, I don't think we'll be getting any closer than the police did to solving this case."

"What are you talking about…"

"I mean that kid was lucky this guy wasn't hungry." The detective responded, walking towards the door.

Tom looked to Uncle Pete and they both looked toward the detective and shook their heads.

"Sorry to bother you, Mr Van," Tom nodded to Uncle Pete. He followed the detective out the door.

Encounter

Mark Deloy

The four-year old girl meandered through the upstairs of the house looking for something to do. She was a beautiful child with long black hair like her mother's and silvery blue eyes. She was wearing her pink jumper today.

It had been overcast all day and now it was beginning to rain steadily. The house was old and slanted slightly to the left when you looked at it from the road. Her grandmother had lived in the Tennessee home her entire life, and in her old age, had not been able to handle the upkeep or routine maintenance. The ancient splintered hardwood floors sometimes caught the child's socks in some places and she's learned the hard way not to drag her feet.

Usually in the summer it was blisteringly hot inside the house, but today with the storm brewing, it had been muggy, but bearable. Krissy followed one of the big orange cats down the stairs and into the sitting room where her grandmother was seated in her plaid recliner eating cookies.

Her mother had dropped her off on her way to work at the diner and picked her up on the way home. Krissy didn't mind staying with her grandmother, but sometimes it got boring. Today with the rain and with Nana watching her stories on the television, Krissy was very bored indeed. She decided that if she couldn't play outside, that she'd ask her Nanna if she could play on the back porch.

"Yes baby, but stay on the porch," the old woman said, handing her an Oreo.

Krissy went into the kitchen to gather up her dolls and her plastic dishes for a tea party. The cats, most of whom lived on the back porch would also make excellent guests. She put everything in her small red wagon and pulled it past her Nanna, who smiled but didn't get up to help her, down the hall, and to the back door. The heavy wooden door was open, as it was most of the time in the summer, and the screen door, which was barely attached to the house stood resting on it's splintered frame. The dirty rust covered screen was torn in several places and the faded green paint was peeling off the wood frame. Krissy pushed the screen door open and then pulled the wagon half way out, wedging the door open so that she could gather her dishes and party guests without going in and out a bunch of times to get everything.

"Don't leave that screen door open Krissy Lynn," her Nanna yelled from the sitting room. "You'll let the flies in."

"OK Nanna," Krissy said looking at the torn screen and smiling as she pulled the last doll out of the wagon and set her down carefully on the porch. She shut the screen door, being careful not to let it slam and began setting up her tea party.

The cats looked sleepily at her from their places on the railing. They were all barn cats that Krissy's grandmother fed scraps to. They had become fat and friendly. There were five of them. Nanna had only gotten around to naming two. Barney and Gomer. Barney was the thinnest of the bunch. Gomer was a cross-eyed Himalayan who was always running into things.

The rain was hammering against the porch roof, but the day was still and no rain had blown onto the porch. It was a perfect cool and dry play area. The boards were even more ragged and splintered than the ones inside the house. The porch used to be painted a bright blue, now the paint had faded and peeled its way to a dull gray. Krissy's grandfather, when he was still alive, had hung a Coca-Cola thermometer on the beam to the left of the porch steps. Now the metal had rusted around the mercury tube, but it still worked. Krissy liked to read it and tell her grandmother how hot it was in the shade and hear her Nanna say "Whoowee child that's hot." Today however the mercury only reached 78 degrees. Krissy's momma had taught her how to count to one hundred and so far the thermometer was the only use that she'd had for counting past ten.

The rain had tapered off some and Krissy looked at the rain puddled yard, wondering when it would be dry enough again for her to go out and play. Her Grandmother's yard was flat for a half acre and then slanted up on a rocky hillside with scattered shrubs, before being engulfed in cedars on the top of the grade. It was much more fun to play here, than in the small yard around her parent's trailer.

There were places to explore and things to discover. There were always animals around to play with. Even Nanna's mule; Hitchcock, was fun to feed and pet. Krissy went back to her tea party and tried to make the best of the dreary day.

Suddenly one of the cats hissed. Krissy looked up. It was Barney. He was growling and hissing at something in the yard. His back was arched and his fur was standing straight up. Krissy looked and saw nothing, just rain and a soggy green lawn. The wind had suddenly picked up and grown colder. Then the other cats began growling and hissing like Barney. Three of them took off over the porch railing and through the rain towards the front of the house, away from whatever it was that scared them. Gomer and Barney stood their ground for a minute, then Barney followed the others and Gomer jumped off the railing and slammed headfirst into the wood at the base of the screen door. He backed up and then leapt through the already torn screen, slicing his stomach and trailing blood into the house. He screeched and it was an awful sound, full of pain and terror.

Krissy looked again out into the yard and at first she still didn't see anything. The clouds and rain had darkened the landscape, making it difficult to see at any distance. Krissy had been looking in the immediate yard. Now she looked up higher towards the rocky hillside and the treeline above it. She spotted movement to the left of a small tree. It was an old woman, or at least Krissy thought that it was a woman. The hag was covered in a black lacy gown that covered her feet and legs. It was dirty and torn in some places and she could see the thing's reddish black flesh underneath, as if a black woman had been dipped in blood. Sleeves covered its arms and hands, flowing freely in the quickening breeze. She wore a brimmed hat, also black, round on top frayed and full of holes. The thing's long gray hair was matted and looked to have large brown spiders crawling around in it and then disappearing beneath it into her gown. The woman's head was down and Krissy couldn't quite see her face. The hag was moving along the hillside and at first Krissy couldn't understand what was wrong about her movements, then the thing moved faster as if realizing that it had an audience. Krissy realized what was so different about the way that she moved. She wasn't stumbling at all on the rocky slippery wet hillside as a normal person would have been. The woman was floating about five inches off the ground.

The breeze now ruffled the bottom of her gown and raised it slightly and now Krissy was sure of what she was seeing. The witch was barefooted and Krissy saw the same dark, blood red flesh on the woman's feet and ankles as they floated freely above the slanted ground. She held a staff, but it never touched the ground either. Instead she used it for balance, holding it out in front of her. Years later when Krissy had gone to the circus for the first time and saw the high wire walkers, she screamed and cried until her mother had to take her home.

The hag apparently hadn't seen her on the porch, and Krissy wanted to keep it that way. The woman glided at a diagonal angle towards the trees. Krissy sat wide eyed and open mouthed, watching, too terrified to move or scream. She just watched, waiting for the thing to reach the woods and glide into the darkness beyond, out of sight, hopefully forever. Just as the thing reached the edge of the woods, she stopped. It seemed like hours. Krissy looking at her hunched over back with her flowing gray, spider-infested hair flowing in the wind, and the hag just standing there as if she were waiting for something. Then Krissy saw her head bob slightly upward, then again and a third time. When the hag turned around Krissy realized what the thing was doing. The hag had floated all the way around now and she was facing Krissy for the first time. Krissy saw her head bob once again. The Witch was sniffing the air. She had caught Krissy's scent on the wind and now she was coming for her. The witch was watching her, sitting frozen on the old paint peeled porch. The witch was even uglier than Krissy had envisioned her before seeing her face. She had the same reddish tinted black skin that covered the rest of her body covering her face, only her face was covered in oozing sores that spilled brown slime onto the front of her gown. The thing's eyes glowed red in the dim storm light and her nose looked broken and cantered off to the left. The skin on the thing's neck was wrinkled and bloodied. The spiders that Krissy had thought lived in her the thing's hair now came crawling out of the wrinkles in her neck.

Krissy tried to scream and all that came out was a small hissing sound. The hag was looking right at her, red eyes glowing. Then the hag tilted her head back and hawked up a wad of something and spat it into her hand. She rubbed her hands together as if she was applying lotion. Krissy could hear her chanting something low and guttural. Then the hag put both of her hands to her mouth, which even at this distance, Krissy could see was filled with razor sharp teeth, and she blew out a breath. Millions of black flies flew out from between the witch's hands. They flew straight at her turning the day to night.

The flies reached the porch and Krissy finally found her voice. She screamed as shrill and as loudly as she ever had. The large hair covered flies were all around her now, in her hair, in her ears, nose and mouth. She spit them out. They tasted like rancid meat. She fished them out of her ears and blew them out of her nose. They were in her clothes now and she could feel them crawling around on her skin. They were on the back of her neck. She was still screaming and flailing her arms around, wondering why her Nanna wasn't coming to help her. She had her eyes shut tight against the crawling invaders. She was spinning around in circles waving her hands and not realizing where her feet were taking her until she felt herself falling.

She fell off the porch and into the mud at the bottom of the stairs, missing the stairs completely on her way down. The good news was that the flies had stopped swarming around her. The bad news was as she wiped the mud from her eyes she could see that the witch was floating down the hillside towards her. Both of the things claw like hand were outstretched now. Her gnarled staff was stowed in some sort of holder on her back.

Krissy's bladder let go and she sat there crying covered in mud. She could still feel the flies on her skin, even though they had all gone from her. The hag got closer, its arms still outstretched, her long bony fingers making grabbing motions in the air. Krissy could see it's mouth clearly now and she had been right about the razor sharp teeth. They seemed to be filed to points. The hag was smiling broadly now at her victory. Then her expression changed.

She hunched down even more than she was and hissed almost like the cats had done earlier at her. The hag was no longer looking at Krissy, but to the porch above her.

Krissy looked and at first she thought that she was looking at some new children that Nanna had taken in to babysit. Then she realized that she was looking right through the two identical girls who were standing hand in hand. The girls had no expression. They had blond ringlets and snow white dresses and they didn't say a word. They only unclasped each other's hand and cupped their own to their mouths much as the witch had done. Instead of black flies coming out from their hands, butterflies swarmed over Krissy's head and straight at the witch who was pulling her gown up to cover her head for protection. She was still hissing, but now she was also screeching and wailing like a scalded cat as the butterflies covered her in a mass of gold, red and blue. She started turning in circles, still screeching and moaning. She turned faster and faster until she was a black blur beneath the insects. Then the soft wet ground beneath her gave way and she bored into the earth, spitting up clumps of grass, soil and mud. Then she was gone. All that was left was a spot in the soil that was slightly raised and had no grass covering it.

Krissy looked to where the two girls had been, and they too were gone along with their golden butterflies. She was still crying thirty seconds later when her Nanna came out, saw her in the mud. At first she started to scold her, then she realized how scared the girl was and pulled her to her instead. Krissy was shaking and began crying hysterically again. Her Nanna brought her inside, gave her a bath, made her some hot cocoa and sat her next to her on the couch. Krissy's grandmother never asked the child what had made her so scared. The look on the child's face and the state that she was in when the old woman came out the door had already told her that she'd been visited. She wondered what she would tell Krissy's mother when she came to pick the child up and found that her hair had gone from jet black to dead white.

BLACK WATER BAYOU

Stanley T. Evans

Down in the Atchafalaya Basin of Louisiana there's a bayou called Black Water. Here, the water and the seasons, not the craziness of the rest of the world, control life. By day, folks are fishing and giving tours to the city people who come to buy trinkets and gawk at nature. The inky black waters and the tall cypress trees hanging full of Spanish moss prove to be a powerful lure. By day, boatloads of people come and go in and out of the swamp. The locals take care of their daily business and go on about their way. When the darkness of night comes creeping into the bayou, folks head for home. You see, a ghost haunts this place and the locals tell the legend still.

Old Willy Mathis had lived in the backwaters of the bayou longer than anyone could remember. The old men playing checkers in front of the sundry store could recall when they were children and Willie was already old. It seemed no one could remember a time when that cranky old man wasn't poling his homemade boat up to the back of the sundry to sell skins, catfish, gator or crayfish. Three generations of owners had been dealing with old Willie. Some spread the rumor that old Willie had made a pact with the devil or was some kind of wizard with his black magic keeping him alive. To the more sensible folks, he was simply as much a part of the swamp as the mosquito or the mud turtle. Willie would pole up to the back dock every Monday, Wednesday and Friday morning. All he ever did was drop off his catch and collect his money. He didn't hang about for idle talk. He didn't seem to have the time for that. Sometimes, he would buy a little coffee and snuff. Other times, he would treat himself to a bag of dry beans and a slab of cured bacon. Most of the time, he would just pole back out into the black waters he called home. Once a year, he'd buy some new clothes. After all those years of miserly living, old Willy Mathis must have some money stashed away. How much money was the subject of many different rumors and rumors can be dangerous things.

One morning, the three Lindale boys were at the sundry when old Willy came to call. They sat out by the dock, smoked their cigarettes and watched old Willy collect his money then pole slowly away.

These young men were ugly and mean like stray dogs raised wild. They had no fear of anyone and even less respect for the law. Their daddy got himself killed by the sheriff while robbing another man's house back when the boys were young. Their mamma was still doing time. She'd tried to shoot the sheriff for killing her husband. This was a family that was mean through and through.

The eldest got himself an idea watching the old man fade into the swamp. It was a full moon that night. That meant they would be able to see without lanterns back in the bayou. He decided to see if the legend of Willy Mathis' money was true. The legend was the old swamp wizard kept his money hid and only took it out on moonlit nights to run his fingers through it. It was a shame for a greedy old man to have all that money and not do anything with it. The Lindale boys all laughed and said they could put all that money to a much better use than mattress filler.

Once the moon was high in the sky, the Lindale boys all met down by the water. They got in their raggedy old flat bottom boat and began poling out into dark swamp floating on that black water. The moon shone eerily through the trees and long hanging tendrils of Spanish moss. Its face shimmered across the mirror of the water's surface. They could hear the night creatures of the swamp out in the water with them. Soft splashes and eddies in the water told the story of the night. They poled on, moving deeper and deeper into the bayou. The eldest smiled to himself. He loved being right. The moon gave them just enough light to make their way through the twist and turns of the slow moving water. A lantern would have let someone know they were coming and they didn't want to do that. They wanted their arrival to be a surprise.

They finally saw a light back in the heart of the bayou. An oil lamp flickered in the distance. They slid quietly across the water towards the floating house. Crazy old Willy could be seen moving about. They poled up quiet as an owl flying over a mouse. They pulled up along the dark side of Willy's place and climbed aboard. Careful as copperheads and twice as deadly, they snuck up on poor old Willy Mathis.

They beat the old man down fast and left him on the floor while they tore his place apart. He'd been fixing a little dinner for himself not rolling in his miserly gains under the full moon. He just lay there on the floor while they shouted and cussed at him but it did no good. They keep pulling things down and tearing things up until they just plain got lucky. They found his money all neatly stuffed in coffee cans and mason jars. They stuffed all that money into an old sack tossed it out in their boat. They picked up poor old Willy Mathis and tied his big iron skillet to his shirt. That unfortunate old man got flung out into the deep black water that had been his home. He disappeared under the water for a long time before he came back up. He spat the dark water at the Lindale boys and started to laugh. He laughed loud and clear. His voice was young and strong. He laughed till the black water sucked him down.

The Lindale boys poled for all they were worth but that laughter stayed with them. Their ears were filled with the sounds of Willy Mathis going down. The moon hid its face behind the clouds. They couldn't see where to go or where to turn. The laughter haunted their every move. They, sweating hard and getting spooked, just kept poling harder. Just as they thought they had hit clear water, boat hit something hard. It felt like a log until they heard the hiss of an angry gator. It bit at the boat and slapped the side with its massive tail. Those Lindale boys screamed and cussed that gator as they poled away from him. The trees were getting closer together and the moss was getting thicker. Tendrils of wet spider web came unseen out of the darkness to snare their whiskered faces. The darkness closed in on them and in a voice loud and clear, that dead old man kept laughing.

They saw headlights pass in the distance. They realized they were way downstream by the overpass. All they had to do was make it to the shore and run up to the highway. They could walk back with their bag of money. They heard the reeds parting as they nosed in. Finally, they heard the scratch of gravel and sand against the bottom of the boat as they hit the shore. They leapt from the boat and ran. They ran as hard as they could. They ran to escape the laughter of that dead old man but it didn't do them any good. They were running in quicksand. They screamed and cussed while they fought to pull themselves out. The Lindale boys screamed and screamed but no one came. They finally took to fighting with each other as the quicksand kept pulling them in deeper and deeper. The last thing anyone of them heard was old Willy Mathis laughing as the gritty black swamp swallowed them down.

That was years ago but if you go down there chasing legends, they say that the quicksand the Lindale boys landed in is always ready to claim any of the unwary. Don't go looking for their ill-gotten gains. The bayou claimed all that money. None of it has ever been found and on certain nights, when the moon is full and bright, if you are out in the Black Water Bayou you can still hear those young men screaming and you can hear old Willie Mathis laugh.

Love's Magic

Donna L. Zeller

Chapter One

Looking at herself in the mirror, Grace was pleased with what she saw. Sighing contentedly, she turned to her best friend Maggie and said, "I feel as if I am walking in a dream cloud."

Maggie almost lost control at that point. She, who had waited patiently for Jonathan, was being passed over for Grace. Of all the luck, she thought.

She knew that she had to say something. Grace was just standing there waiting for her reply. Taking a deep breath and clenching her fists along her side, Maggie said, "I believe we had better join the party. The guests began to arrive a while ago."

"Do promise that you will visit often after Jonathan and I are married. I will miss you so much."

Maggie took Grace's arm and replied, "Of course, my dear. Of course, I will do that."

Grace never noticed the look on Maggie's face as they descended the grand staircase. Her eyes were focused on Jonathan standing next to her parents.

Maggie's thoughts were anything but happy or nice. She had made up her mind to take Jonathan aside and speak to him honestly about her feelings tonight. *I should have done that a long time ago. He knew how I felt about him. How dare he treat me like this!*

Grace's parents greeted them both affectionately. William and Elizabeth Chandler doted on Grace and her older brother, James. They had Grace long after they thought that there was no hope for another child. Along with James, they had spoiled her terribly. In spite of that, Grace had grown up to be very kindhearted and sharing. James, older by twelve years, was working in London as a very successful solicitor. He had recently married his childhood sweetheart, Mary.

Maggie had more or less grown up in the Chandler Mansion. The Chandlers had gone out of their way on more than one occasion to make sure that Maggie knew that she was always welcome. On those infrequent visits to her parents' home, she often returned dispirited. During those difficult times, they felt sorry for her and would try harder to make her feel as if she was part of their family. After a while, the visits to her family stopped altogether.

It was a well-known fact that Maggie's parents didn't want anything to do with raising a child. They were more interested in attending parties that were socially prominent and taking long vacations in the nearby countryside. In spite of their appearances, they lived on barely more than a shoestring in a dilapidated old mansion that they had inherited. The meager staff that they had could hardly take care of the daily chores let alone raise a young child.

Maggie and Grace were about five years old when they met at a birthday party given for a mutual acquaintance. Grace was immediately sorry for Maggie. She noticed that she did not have the attire like the other children and her grooming left something to be desired. Always wanting to help, Grace invited Maggie to her estate for the following weekend. That weekend grew into more weekends which eventually led to Maggie living with the Chandlers on a full-time basis.

Rumors that Maggie had inherited some special skills from her family did not help to endear her to many of Grace's friends. However, Grace was determined to do whatever she could for Maggie. If that meant that some of her friends no longer bothered, she didn't care.

Jonathan had been an older brother of a friend of Grace's. Since their families had often shared holidays together, Grace never thought of Jonathan as much more than another brother. That is, until recently, when Jonathan gently told Grace how he felt. Though she was shocked at the expression of his feelings, she was nonetheless pleased that someone so handsome should take an interest in her. Grace had never taken notice of the fact that she was a real beauty.

On the other hand, Maggie's interest in Jonathan had been instant. The first time that she saw him, she was enchanted. Although she did her best to hide her feelings, her blushing cheeks whenever Jonathan was around gave her away. Jonathan, always the gentleman, had never taken advantage of nor made fun of her in any way.

Jonathan hoped that his interest in Grace would not cause a problem. In fact, he had waited several months before making his intentions known. He knew how much Grace loved Maggie and would not want anything to change between them. He was certain that Maggie had long since outgrown her feelings and that they had been nothing more than a young girl's crush.

He watched as Grace literally floated toward him.

Feeling as if his heart would burst with pride, he reached for her arm to pull her protectively toward him.

Chapter Two

Maggie looked around for an escape. Watching Jonathan and Grace together was not something that she wanted to do. Fortunately, Mrs. Chandler needed something to drink.

"I'll be happy to get that for you," said Maggie. She walked away before anyone had the opportunity to stop her.

She spent as much time as she could near the punch bowl. To add to her misery, the two sisters, Linda and Lucy, were heading in her direction. I must get away before they begin one of their dreary conversations, she thought.

"Well," said Richard, "if it isn't our Maggie."

Maggie literally seethed at his comment. He was one man who she wouldn't so much as dance with let alone show any interest in.

"Maggie?"

"Oh, Richard, how nice to see you. I am just taking some punch to Mrs. Chandler. You will have to excuse me as she is waiting for it."

She was halfway across the dance floor before he could even think of something to say to stop her.

She returned to Mrs. Chandler and handed the glass of punch to her.

"Thank you, Maggie. That was so kind of you."

"No, problem, Mrs. Chandler."

Maggie sat on a nearby chair. She thought that no one noticed that as she turned her head ever so slightly, a beam of light shot across the room, hitting Richard in his back. The action caused Richard to spill his drink down the front of his shirt.

"Oh," he said, "how clumsy of me." Before he could finish his statement, the wait staff was there helping him to clean up. He was still contemplating what caused him to spill his drink as he walked upstairs to change into a fresh shirt.

Maggie hadn't used her skills since she was a young girl. Some had long since been forgotten; however, her unhappiness made her want to lash out at his annoying behavior. Richard was one person who, in her opinion, deserved the punishment. I could have done much worse, she thought.

However, there was no getting around the dinner that would soon be starting. Maggie already knew that she was expected to sit next to Grace, as she had always done. Opposite to them would be Jonathan. My Jonathan, she thought as she surveyed the room.

She felt a little guilty about what she had done to Richard when she saw the Chandlers. She had always been careful around them. As far as Maggie knew, other than some old rumors, they didn't have any idea about her skills; only Grace knew for sure.

As children, they had had some fun with Maggie's abilities. Whenever they didn't want to eat something, it disappeared or, better yet, it spilled on the floor and caused all kinds of commotions. In spite of the resentment that she was feeling about Jonathan, she loved Grace as a sister.

~~~~~

Dinner was excruciatingly painful as she watched Jonathan and Grace. To make matters worse, Richard kept trying to get her attention. Just when she thought that she had had enough, Grace's Father tapped a spoon on the side of his water glass.

He cleared his throat then began his speech. The speech was what Maggie found most humiliating. She sat there stone-faced as she heard him drone on and on about how proud they were to formally announce Grace's engagement to Jonathan.

Afterwards, there was a round of congratulations during which Maggie was able to slip away. Unfortunately, Richard had seen her leave and followed her into the gardens.
~~~~~

"Hey, Maggie!"

She knew who it was without turning around. Humiliated to the point of anger, Maggie did the unthinkable. She lashed her fury with a huge bolt that landed right in front of Richard. Frightened by what had happened he stopped long enough so that she was able to escape into a nearby gazebo.

When Richard regained his senses, he called, "Maggie, Maggie, are you all right?"

Hearing his concern for her angered Maggie. Why can't he leave me alone?

Suddenly, she heard a whisper. She turned around slowly, looking in all areas of the gazebo to see who was there.

"Maggie, Maggie."

She heard it again. Someone was calling her name. She left the gazebo, heading in the direction that it was coming from. Moving as quietly as possible through the rose garden, she stopped every few steps to listen.

Suddenly, there was a soft touch on her shoulder; however, when she turned around, no one was there. Her impatience was growing as she scanned the area for whatever or whoever was whispering her name. There was nothing that she could see.

Then, she heard Richard calling her again and

again. As his footsteps drew nearer, she felt that whatever it was that had been trying to reach her was gone for now.

"Maggie," Richard cried breathlessly, "are you all right?"

She shrugged his hands off of her shoulders and said, "Of course, I am fine. Whatever is the matter with you?"

"I saw something, a light or something in the garden. I was afraid that you had been hurt."

"Richard, please don't be silly. I think that your imagination has run amuck this evening. Come, let's rejoin the party."

Gladly, he took her arm to escort her to the house. Neither one of them noticed that someone was lurking in the bushes.

Chapter Three

Grace was grateful that the party was going so well. Her only problem, if it was one, was that she had not seen Maggie for a while. Just when she was going to go looking for her, she saw them walk through the door. Grace laughed happily as she saw Richard and Maggie together.

Jonathan asked, "What's so funny?"

"Look, over there."

Jonathan saw what she meant and thought, I am

glad that she is with Richard. Perhaps, my concern about her feelings was nothing more than nonsense.

To Maggie's dismay, she heard Grace calling them over to the table.

"Maggie, wherever have you been?" Grace asked with a look of mischief in her eyes.

Maggie had to refrain from answering her the way that she wanted. Instead, she replied, "We went for a walk in the garden. I needed some fresh air."

Richard made no comment about what really happened. Besides, he thought, I am not sure what I saw. He planned to return to the gazebo before leaving to look for some clues. Had Maggie known this, she probably would have made sure to keep an eye on him. In the meantime, Richard was grateful to be near Maggie.

After their return to the party, the rest of the evening passed uneventfully, with Richard attentively standing at Maggie's side. Maggie, of course, did nothing about this as it seemed to make Grace happy.

Later that night, as Grace bid farewell to Jonathan, Richard asked Maggie to walk out onto the veranda with him. Feeling that he was about to ask her something that she did not care to reply to, she feigned a headache. Though he was disappointed, Richard bid her goodnight and left without saying what he had waited so long to say to her.

Meanwhile, Grace and Jonathan were taking a long time to say good night. Each promising the other how deep their love was and making arrangements to be together first thing in the morning.

"It won't be long. I don't want a long engagement," said Jonathan in a voice that told Grace that he really didn't want to let go of her.

Grace's whole body was tingling as she walked up the stairs to the bedroom that she shared with Maggie. There were enough bedrooms in the house; they could have each had their own room. However, they always enjoyed the late night talks, sharing clothing and the companionship of knowing that someone else was there. Maggie was the sister that she had never had.

When she opened the door, she was surprised that Maggie wasn't there. Normally, Grace would have gone searching for her; however, she had seen her with Richard and just assumed that they were still together.

Anyway, after a long evening, she needed to relax. As she prepared a warm bath, she looked around her remembering all of the years that she and Maggie had spent in this room.

~~~~~

Maggie was doing something quite different though. She had managed to return to the garden without anyone seeing her. The voice she had heard calling her name was somehow familiar; yet she couldn't place it. The sound had haunted her throughout the evening. She was determined to find out what was going on.

Unfortunately, Richard had the similar thoughts. He, too, wanted to return to the gardens. In his case, he wanted to find what was causing the eerie glow to appear then disappear.

Neither Richard nor Maggie saw one another as they searched throughout the garden. Maggie was becoming frustrated as she began to accept the fact that the voice that she had heard had disappeared. She was certain that the flash of light that Richard had mentioned was caused by her momentary lapse in judgment when she lashed out at him.

On the other hand, Richard was certain that the glow of light was something else. Little did Maggie know that Richard was very aware of her special skills. He had known for a while that her talents were very much like his. It is only a matter of time before she learns the truth, he thought as he contin-
~~~~~

ued his investigation.

As a last effort to discover what might be causing the sound, she decided to look in the bushes near the edge of the garden. In her zealous effort to look through the thorny hedges where she had last heard the voice, Maggie stumbled and fell.

"Oh, help!" she yelled as she tried to catch herself before tumbling headfirst down the embankment.

Richard heard her and, though he ran as fast as he could, he could not stop her fall.

"Maggie, Maggie," he yelled, "I'll come to you. Don't try to get up."

Although she was in great pain, the anger at hearing his voice gave her strength to stand up on her own and begin the long climb back up the embankment.

Richard was able to get to her when she was about halfway up the hill. Grabbing her arm to help her over a large rock, he asked, "What happened?"

"I was simply out for a walk in the gardens. I live here, remember? I might like to inquire as to what you are doing here!"

"Yes, of course. I was only getting a breath of fresh air before beginning the long drive to my home."

She knew he was lying. What she didn't know was the reason for his lie. She assumed that he was acting as he did because of his feelings for her.

Once again, neither one of them noticed that they were being observed as they left the garden.

Chapter Four

"Where were you?" Grace demanded when Maggie finally returned to the room.

"I was out for a walk," replied Maggie.

If Grace noticed that her reply was a little surly, she didn't say anything. She was too wrapped up in her own happiness to be aware of anyone else's feelings. On the other hand, Maggie didn't care to discuss how she was feeling anyway; especially not with Grace.

To top it all off, I had to run into Richard again, Maggie thought as she drifted into a fitful sleep.

She heard the voice again and again throughout the night. It was beckoning her from the garden. Twice she got up to look out the window. She saw nothing.

Grace slept through it all. When they awoke in the morning, Grace was bright-eyed and in love with the world. In contrast, Maggie looked like she had not slept in a week and didn't care to face anyone or anything.

When Grace asked if anything was wrong, Maggie said that she had a headache. This time, though,

Grace felt that something was wrong and began to ask a few questions. When she didn't receive a reply, she left the room. Knowing that Grace's feelings were more than a little hurt bothered Maggie.

After several minutes of fighting her desire to stay in bed, Maggie got up to get dressed. In doing so, she had to pass in front of the window that faced the garden. From the height of the third floor, she saw someone searching the area around the gazebo. Her anger reached new heights when she recognized that it was Richard.

Dressing quickly, she ran downstairs and was just about ready to open the front door when Mrs. Chandler called her.

"Maggie, my dear, you have a caller."

Maggie walked into the formal living room, wondering who could be visiting so early in the morning. She was not pleased when she saw her parents seated on the sofa.

"Mom, Dad?"

"Hello, Maggie. How are you?" her Mother asked as she walked over to hug her.

Maggie did nothing to return the hug. She looked over her Mother's shoulder to see that her Father was looking at the floor. That usually means there is something wrong. What do they want from me now? she wondered.

Mrs. Chandler had thoughtfully ordered some coffee and crescents to be brought in. After the maid had dutifully placed everything on a small coffee table, Mrs. Chandler excused herself saying that she had a few things to take care of.

That left Maggie alone with her parents which was something she did not want. She knew them too well. They were not here to inquire about her well-being.

Looking at them with cold eyes, she asked, "What do you want?"

"We just wanted to see our daughter. It has been a while," her Mother replied with what Maggie knew were fake tears in her eyes.

"All right. I'll play along. It is wonderful to see the two of you again. I have missed you."

For the first time since she had entered the room, Maggie's Father joined the conversation saying, "Don't talk to your Mother like that!"

"Whatever!" replied Maggie.

Unaware that Richard was listening from the front porch, Maggie asked, "What do you want? What are you really doing here?"

Richard listened attentively wanting to know, too, what they wanted. He was aware that, had the Chandlers not taken Maggie in, she probably would have ended up in much less fortunate circumstances.

In spite of knowing her parents reputation, even he was shocked when they asked Maggie for help with their current situation. Fortunately, they had never learned the full scope of Maggie's special skills and didn't realize the powers that she had that could have changed their circumstances drastically. Maggie, too, was smart enough never to divulge that she could have done something for them. To the best of his knowledge, no one, maybe not even Maggie, was aware of who she really was.

Maggie was reeling from the impact of their request when Richard entered the room, greeting everyone jovially. Although Maggie was not pleased with Richard's presence, she didn't ask him to leave. Even though he doesn't have a clue as to what is happening here, at least I have someone on my side, she thought as she tried to think of a way to get away from her parents without causing a scene.

Richard was a step ahead of her on that thought and said, "Maggie, you promised to join me for a walk this morning. Well, here I am!"

Maggie, though she loathed having to spend time with Richard, was grateful for the excuse that he was providing. She had no idea that he knew all there was to know about her. Maggie just figured that he had sensed an uncomfortable situation and was being his usual gallant self.

Maggie replied, "Oh, yes. I almost forgot. We had better leave right now as I promised Grace that I would do something with her later on."

Before her parents had a chance to do or say anything, Richard and Maggie were well on their way toward the garden. Both had very different reasons for wanting to return there.

Chapter Five

After they realized that Maggie had managed to get away before they had the opportunity to ask the all important question, her parents began to argue.

Celia was livid. "You should have stopped her!"

"Me!" cried Bill, "Why is it always me when something doesn't happen your way?"

As soon as they realized that they were shouting loud enough for the entire house to overhear what they were saying, they quieted down immediately. They left without ever saying a word to Elizabeth Chandler. She wasn't at all surprised when she saw them racing down the driveway in the car that they probably couldn't afford.

In the meantime, Maggie knew that Richard was leading her back to the gazebo. She suddenly knew, without being told, that he had some kind of insight to more than she ever imagined. Her only hope was that she would be able to slip away from him long enough to try to find the source of the whispering. She was positive that he hadn't heard it.

"Come on, Maggie," called Richard as he ran the last couple of yards to the gazebo. Just in case there was any evidence that someone had been there, he wanted to reach it first. The whispering voice that was calling Maggie's name the night before had haunted him so much that he hadn't been able to sleep. He was beginning to get irritable as a result.

Maggie wanted nothing to do with following Richard to the gazebo. She wanted to continue her search through the bushes. She waited until his back was turned again then, without telling him, she ran in the opposite direction.

Maggie was breathless when she reached the point that she had fallen from the night before. Looking down at the steep hill, she wondered how she had managed not to hurt herself.

When Richard noticed that she had vanished, he knew exactly where to look for her. Having given some thought to the situation, he had decided that if she did go to the rose bushes then she must have heard the voice there, too. With that in mind, he chose to watch her from behind a nearby garden statue. He would be able to see and hear anything from there without scaring aware whoever else was out there.

Fortunately, Maggie did not notice Richard maintaining his vigilance over her. If she would have seen him, she would not have continued her pursuit. Thinking that she was alone, Maggie began to look through every bush and around every statue. At the end of a painstakingly long hour, she gave up. She was frustrated and tired to the point of wanting to scream.

Noticing the agitated look on her face, Richard thought that it was about time to remind her that he was there. He ran back to the gazebo then began calling her name again and again. Maggie, at long last, answered him. He ran to her as if finally finding her after a long search.

"Maggie, where have you been?"

"I was looking at the rose bushes. Where have you been?"

Richard continued the charade by replying, "I was waiting for you in the gazebo."

"Anyway, we'll have to leave," said Maggie, "I have to meet Grace in a half hour. Come on, I'll walk you to your car."

Richard knew he couldn't delay his departure for much longer. All he could do, for now, would be to let her walk him to his car. After that he would have to at least pretend to leave. He knew of a back road around the property. From there, he could return to the garden without her ever being the wiser. He would do that later, at dusk. He was certain that the night hours had something to do with the whispering voice.

He was beginning to feel that Maggie had more powers than she realized. That concerned him. She could possibly do harm to herself or someone else if she wasn't careful. He smiled at the thought that she would probably be more than happy to cause him some pain, if she knew the range of her abilities.

After he left, Maggie went back to the house. She was relieved to learn that her parents had left right after she did. Mrs. Chandler managed to stop her long enough to attempt to speak to her about her relationship with her parents. As always, Maggie wanted nothing to do with what she was saying. The conversation was ended abruptly, when Maggie used her meeting with Grace as an excuse to make a polite exit. Though Mrs. Chandler knew that she had no alternative but allow Maggie to go, she made a mental note to speak with her about her issues with her parents in the next few days.

Chapter Six

"Maggie!"

Maggie heard Grace's voice before she saw her. She was glad that they were having lunch together. Maggie knew without a doubt that the situation with Jonathan would change a lot of things between her and Grace. If possible, she wanted to try to help Grace to understand that Jonathan belonged to her. There was something that was almost familiar about him. It was as if they had been together before, sometime or somewhere else.

"Grace!"

"Maggie, I was able to get reservations at our The Marble Restaurant. Can you believe that?"

"We haven't been there together in a long time," replied Maggie. She didn't mention that was where she had first seen Grace and Jonathan together sitting, holding hands in a corner booth.

When they walked in the front door, her eyes were drawn to that booth. She almost wanted to scream when she realized that was where the waiter was going to seat them. With as much calm as she could muster, Maggie slid into her side of the booth. This is exactly where Jonathan sat. I can almost feel him next to me, she thought.

"What are you going to have?" asked Grace.

"Huh? Oh, probably my usual," replied Maggie.

Grace noticed that Maggie was not talking much so she asked her if she had a good time with Richard. Maggie's reply didn't tell her much of anything. She knew from her Mother that Maggie had had another visit from her parents. It was a surprise to everyone that they seemed to be showing up a little more frequently these days. Grace attributed her being so quiet to that.

After they placed their order, they talked about the many things that they shared over the years. When the topic moved to the future, Grace could not stop talking about Jonathan. Maggie almost choked on a sip of tea when Grace asked her if there was any possibility of a serious relationship with Richard.

Maggie knew then that somehow she would have to speak with Jonathan. She was certain that when he knew her true feelings that he would want to be with her. Together, they would let Grace know gently. We must tell her soon. She is getting far too excited about the wedding. The last thing that I want is to have Grace hurt, Maggie thought as she bit into her sandwich.

Grace was doing some thinking, too. She wondered if Maggie still had feelings for Jonathan. Of course, Maggie had told her how she felt but that was a long, long time ago. Grace thought, I think her behavior lately is due to her parents' sudden reappearance in her life. Besides, she seems to be happy for Jonathan and me.

Later, as they were walking down the boulevard, Grace asked Maggie something that they hadn't talked about in a long time. Maggie took a long time to reply. When she did, she said, "I really don't know much about my powers. Other than the few times that you and I had some fun with them when we were young, I haven't really used them."

Grace didn't want to tell Maggie that she had seen the bolt that had zapped Richard, causing him to spill his drink, at the dinner. She had been on the verge of telling Maggie to stop when she lost sight of both of them that evening.

For now, she accepted Maggie's explanation. She had no other choice; however, she planned to talk to her again about it. Grace had also heard the whispering at night. The voice was calling her, too.

Chapter Seven

It was two a.m. when they heard the whispering voice. This time, there was no mistake. It was calling to both of them. Without any hesitation, they dressed and ran outside to the garden.

Grace whispered, "It is coming from over here."

Maggie followed her to the now familiar area of the rose bushes. Once again, there was no sign of anything or anyone.

Grace insisted that they check the entire garden. "Just to make sure that there really isn't anything out here. You know, it might just be the wind."

Maggie replied, "I don't think that the wind would be able to pronounce our names quite so clearly."

Grace had to agree. Both women almost screamed when they saw a shadow move behind the large oak tree.

"It's Richard! Whatever are you doing here?" asked Grace.

Richard looked at Maggie, first. It was apparent that she was angry with him. Grace appeared to be surprised by his presence but also seemed to be relieved to have him there. Richard wasn't sure of what to do or to say next.

Maggie had it with Richard always showing up and she was about to let him know it.

That's when it happened. They all heard it. The voice was distinctly calling to them from the bottom of the hill. Richard signaled to them to follow him quietly. As they edged their way to the crest of the hill, the voice became louder.

Just as suddenly, it was gone. There wasn't a sound to be heard in the stillness of the night. The three of them wandered around the garden for a while before deciding to give up.

"I don't know," said Maggie, "this may be just the wind blowing through the trees as Grace suggested."

Richard looked at her sadly. He knew who it was and why he was there. Grace didn't say a word. She was beginning to feel that there was some connection between Maggie's special powers and whatever was happening in the garden.

Given the late hour, Richard suggested that they all get some sleep. Grace offered the use of the guest house. "It is too late for you to drive home."

He, of course, accepted the invitation. One reason was because he was very tired; however, the more pressing reason was to stay close to Maggie and Grace. While he had an inclination as to what was going on; he didn't understand why.

The three of them slept late the next morning. While they were having a late brunch on the patio, Richard listened as Grace and Maggie plotted their next move. He wanted to be part of whatever they decided to do. Staying in the guest house was the only way that would happen.

Later, when Maggie went to the kitchen for more coffee, he asked Grace if there was a problem with his using the guest house for a while. Fortunately, she never asked his motive. Grace assumed that it was due to his interest in Maggie and agreed heartily to the idea.

When Maggie learned of the arrangement, she let Richard know exactly how she felt about his living there. Grace felt terrible to have caused such a bitter quarrel and tried her best to calm the situation.

"Maggie, you are being most unreasonable," he told her during one brief lull in the tirade of insults.

Maggie fired back at him. "You are getting to be bothersome!"

"Maggie," he called as she left to go to her room.

To complicate matters more, she noticed that her parents' car was parked in the driveway. Richard and Grace saw it, too.

Chapter Eight

She couldn't avoid them. They were seated, once again, in the parlor. Trying her best to sneak past them, she couldn't avoid the meeting when Elizabeth Chandler called her into the room.

"Yes," said Maggie as politely as possible.

"Your parents are here, my dear."

"I see them."

"They wish to speak to you."

"If you think that is what I should do, then I will do it."

Elizabeth thought for a few minutes before replying calmly, "Yes, dear, I do think that you should give them an opportunity to say what they have come to say."

Without further argument, Maggie sat down opposite her parents on a corner chair. The fact that the chair faced the garden was just another coincidence to Maggie. In the growing perplexity of her life, she was tired of trying to figure things out.

Surprisingly, her Father spoke first. "You have done very well for yourself, Maggie."

Maggie didn't care to reply. They all knew that if it hadn't been for the Chandlers' love, she would not have been so fortunate.

Her Mother spoke next. Maggie had surmised correctly what they were there for.

"We need your help, Maggie."

Maggie asked, "What is it that you think I can do for you?"

"Your skills, Maggie. They have come to you through the generations. Unfortunately, I misused mine in one errant act and they are gone from me.

You, though, can do whatever you want."

Maggie thought for a long time before asking, "I will do one thing for you then you must promise that in return you will both never see me again."

Celia looked at her miserably, then said, "Please don't ask that."

Her Father added, "We do love you. It hasn't been easy for us either."

Maggie replied vehemently, "As I said, I will help you this one time then please leave me alone."

Fortunately for Maggie, it didn't take her parents long to agree to her demands. Neither Celia nor Bill had any desire to continue living as they did. They knew that Maggie was the one hope that they had.

"When?" asked Maggie.

"As soon as possible."

Her parents waited as Maggie struggled with the choice that she had to make. When she did comply with their wishes, there was no sign that she had used her skills. There weren't any light or sound displays. No, Maggie simply did what she had to do.

Afterwards, Maggie explained as patiently as possible what she had accomplished. Yes, the mansion had been fixed; however, there was more work to be done. Her parents would have to follow up on whatever else they wanted to repair. Also, there would be enough money now; however, there was an account with a fixed income in their names. That account would be replenished at the first of every month. They were not to contact her to plead for anything else.

When Bill and Celia understood the limited generosity that their daughter had bestowed, they became adamant in requesting more.

"Who do you think you are? You wouldn't have the powers if it weren't for me!" demanded Celia.

Maggie replied quietly, "I don't care where they are from. To be honest with you, I don't care about the mystical powers at all. In fact, I often wished that I had been born without them."

It was a long time before Celia and Bill realized that Maggie was firm in her decision. There was no amount of berating or pleading that would make her change her mind. Without so much as a farewell, they left. Maggie never saw them again after that day.

Chapter Nine

When they least expected it, the voice returned again. This time, they couldn't ignore that it was eerily familiar. As the three of them searched the garden, the realization as to who the voice belonged to dawned on Grace and Maggie at the same time.

"It sounds like Jonathan!"

Richard didn't want to admit it but it definitely sounded like Jonathan. He wasn't sure what he was doing there but they were about to find out.

They had just reached the top of the hill when they heard Jonathan calling to them from the gazebo.

"How could that be?" asked Grace as they turned to see Jonathan running toward them.

"If you are here, who is that down there?" asked Maggie.

Richard knew. He had heard the story. He didn't know until now that it was true.

Jonathan reached them, breathlessly begging them to wait. He turned to Grace and said, "Please try to understand, darling. This is not of my doing."

"Whatever are you trying to say?" asked Grace.

They heard it again. The whispering was louder now.

"Who is down there?" demanded Maggie.

Jonathan turned to Maggie now. "You may want to see for yourself."

The four of them peered over the large boulder. None of them said a word. The apparition, or whatever it was, looked exactly like Jonathan.

Grace asked, "Who is that, Jonathan?"

"It is Michael. He appears now and then. I am afraid that is who Maggie really fell in love with so long ago. It was he who visited with the two of you that fateful day."

"Michael," whispered Maggie.

"Yes, my love?"

Grace, Jonathan and Richard stood by silently as they watched the recognition grow on Maggie's face.

"It is you. You are the one who I met."

Michael smiled. "That is true."

Every detail was becoming clear to her now. She had often sensed a slight difference in Jonathan or rather the person she thought of as him.

She said quietly, "It is you who is there when I feel the attraction. It is as if we have been together always."

"Yes."

Jonathan couldn't remain quiet any longer. He said, "As usual, Michael, you have caused some confusion!"

"Ah, brother of mine, of course I have. But I couldn't resist."

Jonathan laughed and replied, "I know you all too well. The idea of you resisting temptation would not be normal. Whatever will happen now?"

Michael looked at Maggie then. "She will have a decision to make. If she comes with me, she will have to leave all that is familiar. I, in turn, promise to love her as she has never been loved before."

Maggie knew her answer before he had finished speaking. The scene was not unfamiliar to her. She had been here before in her dreams. Only, this time it was real.

Turning to Grace, Richard and Jonathan, she looked at them and said, "I will return as often as possible. I will miss all of you terribly. Richard?"

Richard's reply was the most surprising, "I am your cousin, Maggie. Had you not been so distraught, you would have noticed our common ways."

She smiled at him knowingly then turned to Grace and said, "I shall miss you."

"And, I shall miss you, too. Will you be able to return whenever you want?"

Michael had moved to her side by then and answered for her. "Yes, she may move from one realm to the next whenever she desires." Then, he added with an unmistakable smile, "I will try not to be too lonely when she is gone from my side."

Maggie held onto Grace, Jonathan and Richard for a long time. Michael waited patiently until the time was right. When the winds blew gently and as the moon moved behind the clouds, Michael took her gently with him.

IF I HAD A HUNDRED TONGUES

Barry Baldwin

Although he did not indulge in whimsy about gin pahits on the verandah or the sun being over the yardarm or other such Maughamesqueries, the professor did not take his first drink of the day until precisely six o'clock. It never varied — a modest measure of whatever brand of bourbon was cheapest at the liquor store that week, without water or ice — and was followed by three more, every hour on the hour, after which he would put away the bottle, wash and dry the glass, go through the physical maneuvers that converted his couch into a bed, and retreat without chemical aid into an always dreamless sleep.

On this particular evening, it came into his mind that over all the years of vespertine tippling there had never been anyone else present to pour or be poured for. The reflection vaguely disquieted him, not for what it implied but because it had entered his being at all. He sought to dispel it by — an event without parallel — draining his first hour's ration in a single gulp, sitting down with more than usual emphasis in the armchair that was almost as old as himself, and picking up the antique volume that was the centre of his furnishings and his evening hours. Virgil's Aeneid. Not the dark blue Oxford Text of Sir Roger Mynors or the caerulean Teubner from Leipzig-Stuttgart that he would have used with an advanced class, though he was rarely assigned these, but the edition of G.V. Guellius issued from the Plantine Press at Antwerp in 1576.

This treasure was not his, although he might have said it was to a visitor, had he ever had one. It belonged to the Rare Books Collection of the university. His head of department had long ago arranged for him to have permanent loan of it, partly to irk the Special Acquisitions Supervisor — an old enemy — but mainly to establish a hold ('Refuse to teach that first-year section and the Virgil goes back') over one whose opacity when it came to academic or administrative ambition he found so far beyond understanding as to be a running sore of unease.

He opened the book, taking pleasure as always from its foxed but still firm pages, a reproach to modern flimsiness, still more so to the featureless discs and screens which he was aware other men in his department — he did not easily admit the notions of women and colleagues — would be staring at in other rooms, and turned to the passage that was his favourite, all the more so after the events of that morning. Book Four, verses 173-197, the personification of Gossip or Rumour spreading throughout Carthage the tale of what had transpired carnally and maritally between Queen Dido and the pious prince Aeneas in their African cave, setting in motion the chain of circumstances that would culminate in her self-immolation. Not every editor's choice. That doughty Victorian, T.E. Page, had thundered against it in the old MacMillan 'red' as being grotesque and ludicrous.

The professor had read this aloud that morning to his Great Masterpieces of European Literature class, a motley crew of already stale freshmen and others looking for a Mickey Mouse course or just making up their final load for graduation. He had intoned it first in Latin, which meant nothing to them, then in an English translation of his own making. Not verse, there was poetry in his soul but none in his pen, an obstetric lack that had shaped his life in ways his limited powers of introspection did not always fathom, but in a prose that older generations would have called manly:

Rumour of all evils the most fleet. Speed feeds her strength, she gains vigour as she goes; small at first from fear, she soon ascends to heaven and treads the earth with head veiled in the clouds, a monster awful and huge, with many feathers and as many eyes, mouths, and ears. By night she flies through the gloom, hissing, and drops not her eyes in slumber; by day she perches upon lofty towers and affrights great cities, exulting in gossip, singing alike of fact and falsehood.

He hadn't planned to do this. His lectures were famously dry, lacking the obtruded humour and rehearsed spontaneous 'rapping' with audiences that won Best Teacher Awards for others. He provided basic biography, resisting novelettish reconstructions, historical background, and not too long lists of the best books — articles didn't come into the world of the introductory survey. The worst ones, too. Here, he had once become quite lively, observing of a particular tome that it had spoiled a precious gap in our knowledge. No one had laughed, and the experiment was not repeated.

Aware that all eyes were resting curiously upon him and that no notes were being scratched or in these lap-topped days punched out, he announced that what they had just heard was perhaps one of the greatest moments in civilised literature. He had not planned to say this either. As with many things in his life, it sprang from a sudden bookish recollection, in this case a once well known story of the austere A.E. Housman, notorious for denying any connection between taste and learning, who had upon a unique occasion shocked his Cambridge audience by admitting to the beauty of Horace's ode on the coming of spring.

At the end of the class, a girl came up to him. He instinctively pushed the upright lectern forward to gain more distance between them. She wore clothes that were strange both separately and together, creating an effect as variegated as the goddess he had just described. He thought she might be going to denounce Virgil, and so himself, for blatant sexual stereotyping in this picture of Gossip as a woman; such scenes were ever more common in the university's lecture halls. But, 'you brought her alive,' she said, and was gone before he could respond.

Reverently placing the book pages face downward across his knees, he leaned back and, closing his eyes, reiterated the words, first to himself and then aloud: you brought her alive, you brought her alive. Whereupon his sense of achievement elided into awareness of a persistent hissing sound. The new second-hand — the oxymoron appealed — coffee percolator must be acting up again…

'You brought me alive.'

His eyes followed his ears in opening to the new labio-nasal pronoun. Rumour was there, in front of him, with him, in smallish state but flickeringly multiform as Virgil had created her.

Another man would have jumped up, cried out, perhaps fainted. The professor decided that this was some kind of prank. A stunt orchestrated by the girl in strange clothes, cooked up no doubt with the fraternity brothers who, he recalled, were at present engaged in their annually vexatious charity week. It would not have been hard for them to bribe a key to his apartment out of the building manager who had hated him ever since that first Christmas when he had declined to give the expected seasonal tip.

He thought to baffle the impostor with a touch of humour not attempted since the failed bibliographical epigram. What a pity he had not resurrected Cassandra instead of Rumour. Using her predictions, he could have made a fortune on the race tracks.

The hissing intensified, but the answer came clear. 'Predictions which, as all know, were believed by no mortals. Cassandra was but a speck. I am everywhere at every time. I recreate the past, I reshape the present, I recast the future. All history is gossip…'

These last four words cracked the professorial carapace. How likely was it that some fraternity type would be so well acquainted with both mythology and the aphorisms of Oscar Wilde? He would have spoken again, but whoever or whatever it was in front of him seemed suddenly to expand in size and anticipate his intended question:

Where earth, sky, and sea meet in the centre of the world, there dwell I upon a hill in an always-open palace with a thousand apertures and entrances beyond number, a place of echoing brass that repeats and hurls back the sounds it hears. A whole host lives here, they come and go in shadowy throng, this way and that, some spill their tales into idle ears, others bear to others what they have heard, the story grows as each new teller adds to what has been told.

His already damaged equanimity crumbled. It was surely inconceivable that any impersonator could so fluently reproduce this Ovidian account of the Palace of Rumour. Not even the girl from his class. They did not read the Metamorphoses and in such a course no candidate would venture beyond the prescribed texts.

Another aphorism occurred to him. The Church Father Tertullian: 'credo quia absurdum,' — I believe because it is unbelievable. Again before he could speak the figure was in advance and in a rise and fall and rush of sounds and words painted the picture of a maiden and her desires, a maiden whom he knew but might know better, and of a man whom she and he knew but in different ways, a man whom by knowing which he might better know and who might better know him.

The professor had closed his eyes in the course of this outpouring, the easier to follow it. When it ended and he re-opened them, he was alone.

His first instinct, even now, was to check the level of his whisky bottle. Had he somehow extended his dosage and overdrunk to the point of hallucination? No. Had an intruder tampered with its contents, infusing some brain-addling substance? But the bottle had been a new one, purchased only hours ago, the seal unbroken until its six o'clock defloration.

What he had heard caused him no pondering. The maiden must be the girl in his class, as evidently strange in her desires as in her clothes since he was their object. The man was just as clearly his head of department. No doubt he had interviewed the girl, approved her programme, signed her forms, plied her with wine and cheese at one of the faculty-student receptions the professor himself never attended. He was familiar with the muted but persistent swirl of stories about the head's habitual failure to meet his classes, his cavalier way with expense accounts and travel funds, a reputation-making article said by a sharp-eyed junior sessional to have been plagiarised from a century-old German original: not, however, with the details of faculty wives and undergraduate girls which Rumour had integrated into her effusion.

The second option, considered first in Homeric fashion, was straightforward. A brisk confrontation with the head would at once gain him a permanent upper-hand in matters of course load, priority in the doling-out of research grants, and the other large and small holy grails of academic life which he had previously assumed beyond his grasp and so not sought after.

The issue of the girl was more complex. He had never occupied a bed with a member of either sex, a state of affairs more common than is generally admitted, though in his case it was owed to choice rather than circumstance. As to why she should desire him, finding it beyond reason, he fell back on Virgil: 'varium et mutabile semper femina,' — a windfane changabil huf puffe always is a wooman, in the wild words of the Elizabethan translator Stanyhurst. He was not actively drawn towards reciprocation of the girl's desires; it had been snowing in his heart for too long. And yet, he thought, observing with unwonted pleasure that the clock sanctioned replenishment of his glass, it might be of interest to sample the business once. Experience is a teacher, the Romans had been fond of saying. And he recognised that in a bed not only bodies are shared; the girl might know more to his advantage about the head than himself.

His opening gambit was to detain the girl after his next lecture and invite her to join him for luncheon — he disdained the apocope 'lunch' — that they might discuss Rumour. She accepted in a manner that was offhand verging upon listlessness. He was left with no idea of how she had interpreted the offer, but ascribed this to his lack of dealing with other people's emotions. His chosen venue was the Faculty Club. The idea was that by being witnessed in such open display they, or at least he, would obviate suspicion. He was unaware of the new way of thinking which equates joint public appearance with private entanglement. Oblivious to this, less so to the fact that her clothes, as strange as ever, were a major focal point, he derived a quantum of satisfaction from the way they were looked at as he led her to a corner table in the dining room, its little green-shaded lamp the only illumination.

By the end of their luncheon, he understood less rather than more why she had accepted his invitation. Of her supposed desire, there was no sign, but again he put this down to his own ignorance of such manifestations. Yet she did not demur at the proposal to have dinner at his apartment, though appeared to have some trouble suppressing a smile when he added that it would be an opportunity for her to see his Virgil.

Dinner was a meal the professor normally eschewed. He chose some 'gourmet specials' from the supermarket and left them grimly defrosting on a kitchen counter. He also sought out a remote bookstore where no one knew him and purchased an erotic manual, preferring to the astonishingly lurid contemporary ones an old-fashioned treatise with muddy diagrams adorned by discreet Latin nouns. He placed this in a conspicuous spot on his book shelves,having read that if you leave a guest alone in a room, the first thing they will always do is inspect your library.

The girl arrived with unexpected punctuality, in clothes that were now strangely conventional rather than strangely strange. She refused all alcoholic choices, agreed to a tonic water, looked wordlessly at the proffered Virgil, and was duly left by herself while he reversed into the kitchen to — as he put it — attend to matters. When he came back to announce the meal, she had vanished.

On balance, he was relieved, though did think he might give her the lowest grade compatible with justice in the Great Masterpieces course, something that could in itself (he had heard tell) lead to renewed possibilities. Nor was he perturbed by this suggestion of Rumour's fallibility. Quite the contrary. Virgil was very clear that she sang alike of fact and falsehood. He was very much more concerned that the goddess should have it right about the head of department.

Which, as it fell out, she had. But the essence of gossip is to create situations, not resolve them. At the planned confrontation, the professor set out his charge sheet and demands, to which the head, silent and immobile through this litany, replied without preamble or raising of voice, 'Next semester you'll have a double course load, all freshman surveys. I'll be figuring out some more committees for you to be on. You can forget about any chance of a sabbatical...'

The door opened without a knock. The girl looked

in; she was back in her strange finery. The head gave her a brief glance. She closed the door without a word. 'Oh yes,' he went on as though there had been no interruption, 'one squawk out of you about anything and she'll have you up on a sexual harrassment charge at warp nine speed. Folks around the department have been practically lining up to tell me about seeing the two of you at the Club, and I know all about you getting her up to your place and trying to feed her liquor and the rest.'

As the professor was making his exit, having offered thanks for the appointment, the head called after him, 'One more thing. I want the Virgil here on my desk by nine o'clock tomorrow morning. That deal's off.'

It was more than a week before they found him, it being now mid-semester break with no classes, and in any event no one ever thought about where the professor was or what he was doing, outside regular duties. A methodical search in the library had yielded a book which was adequately instructive on how to calculate the required drop and the exact position of the rope under the angle of the left jaw — under the right, it slips round throwing the neck forward and so causes protracted strangulation.

The relative lack of putrefaction due to the cold

temperature at which he kept his apartment in all seasons was offset by the lingering odour of the excrement engendered by the relaxation of the bowels that accompanies human suspension voluntary or otherwise from a rope.

The police officers who had been admitted by a grumbling building manager found no note. The Virgil was never found either. Its loss caused more grief to the head than that of the professor, not least though not only because of the uncomfortable hour it cost him with the Special Acquisitions Supervisor. He expressed formal regrets to the press and delivered a markedly spare eulogy at the thinly attended memorial service that the university administration could find no way of avoiding. He ended with Virgil's line on those sad souls who in innocence wreak their own deaths. The head and the girl were married some months later. There were any number of interpretations of this event, none correct.

What none of the gossipry knew and what lay beyond invention was that just after the professor kicked over the stool and was launched into wherever it is we go, one corner of the room filled with a strange sartorial immanence that was both dependent upon and autonomous from the faint hissing noise in the other.

THE WISH

Rob Rosen

Sally sat at her sewing machine and sighed.

"Wow," she said, once she realized her actions were also a tongue twister. "How very strange. Though Sally's sighing was fairly standard by that point.

To earn extra needed money, Sally sewed. Sally sewed for the local dry cleaner. Sally sewed for the community playhouse. And Sally certainly sewed for her family. "No use buying it when I can make it," she frequently said to anyone that asked. So for all of these reasons, Sally sewed, and then frequently sighed.

"I sure do wish I didn't have to sew," she said while looking down at her fingers, which were vivid red and as nicked and dinged as her old sewing machine.

Just then, a crack of thunder boomed overhead and a bright light appeared directly in front of her. The light started as a swirling mass about as big as a watermelon and slowly grew to Sally's size, until out of the eddy of light appeared a woman dressed all in white.

"My goodness," Sally gasped. "Who're you?"

"I, my dear, am here to grant you your wish," the strange woman chirped. A wand then magically appeared out of thin air.

"Are you my Fairy Godmother?"

"Not exactly. The Godmother Union is on strike. I'm more of a temporary, um, well, I'm a…"

"A scab." Sally finished her sentence.

"I like to think of it as more of a fill-in gig, if you don't mind."

Sally pondered the strange woman and her statement, and then asked, "Does the wand work?"

The woman nodded and smiled.

"Fine," Sally finally said. "Who am I to judge, anyway?"

"Righteeo, then. Let's give this baby a whirl."

"You have done this wish making business before, haven't you?"

"I've been amply trained and have completely read the manual. Not to fear my dear."

"So you've done this before?" Sally felt the reiteration necessary. The woman didn't exactly inspire confidence.

"Well, you'll be my first human, but I've been

assured that there's little to no difference between humans and mice."

"Besides the fact that mice can't sew."

"Quite. Anyway, take it or leave it, hon. I'm on a tight schedule, what with having to fill in for three Godmothers today.

"No, no. I'll take it. Don't get your panties in a wad. Just making sure," Sally said as she stood up from her sewing machine. "Shoot!" she added, as she shut her eyes and extended her arms and hands out from her sides.

"Fine. Here goes," the woman said, and Sally squinted her eyes open a tad to watch.

Again the glow appeared, haloing the woman and growing more intense by the second, until, all at once, a great shaft of light coursed through the wand and struck Sally dead on.

"Is that it?" Sally said, feeling just a tad dizzy, but otherwise normal.

"What were you expecting? Special effects cost extra. That's one of the strike disputes. Anyway, you got your wish. Now, if you don't mind, there's a girl and a toad, well, it's along story, so ta ta, sweetie. Hope you eeenjooooy iiit…" And as she gradually faded back into the thin air she came in, a wry smile appeared on her face, causing Sally to suddenly shudder.

"Something about that didn't seem quite right," Sally said, perhaps stating the utmost understatement of the century. "And what's with all the tongue twister's today?"

Anyway, something was most definitely different. Sally's sewing machine was nowhere in sight. Sally looked high and low, but it was gone. And there was something else more ominous that sent a shiver down Sally's spine: silence. There was no noise in the house. Or in the neighborhood. Or anywhere, for that matter.

"Uh oh," Sally said. "That can't be good."

She went running around her house, and outside, and down the street, and all around her block, but there was nothing. Not a peep. Not a sound. Not a person to be found. "Oh no, Sally said. Now I'm in rhyme too."

Sally sat and thought about her wish. "I wished I didn't have to sew, and without any people, my wish came true. Damn that Fairy Godmother scab. I should have known better than to trust a rookie."

Just then, as before, a crack of thunder boomed overhead and a bright light appeared directly in front of her. "Oh no, not again," she said. But this time a man appeared out of the swirl of light. A very small man, at that.

"What, a Fairy Godfather now?" Sally asked.

"Nope, guess again. Actually, with the strike still in full force, let's just skip the guessing and go right to the answers. I'm a sprite. We're filling in now until the union can reach an agreement. The woman that was here before was a plant. Seems the Godmothers thought it would bode well for them if their replacements, er, screwed up here and there."

"Here especially," Sally interjected.

"Apparently, but I do have the power to undo her magic. If that is what you desire."

"Well, I do miss my family, but what about another wish. I mean I do have one coming to me, right?"

"Yes, fine, just be quick about it. I'm running late, I have a date, I simply cannot, must not wait."

"Oh no, no more rhymes or tongue twisters, just a simple wish will suffice."

Sally made her wish and the little man glowed a brilliant, white light that grew and grew and grew, until it surrounded them both. Then it grew even brighter and larger in scope, enveloping the entire neighborhood and beyond. And then, as suddenly as it appeared, it vanished, leaving only Sally and her neighborhood in its wake. No sprite. No bright light. And, most importantly, no silence. There was, to Sally's great delight, the noise of children all around her; one of which was her own.

"Hi mama," shouted her son. "What are you doing out here?"

"It's a long story, Billy. And mommy's got a lot of work to d…" But before Sally could finish her sentence, she realized that, if all went as planned, she'd have all the time in the world to spend with her son. "Be right back Billy, you wait right here."

And with that, she was off and running back to her house. The noise of the sewing machine was the first thing she noticed. The second was the replacement Fairy Godmother.

"Ah," Sally said. "Now that was a good wish."

"Speak for yourself, honey," the defrocked fraud replied.

"I am," Sally said, "And now, since I finally have some spare time, I'm going out to play with my son. The extra spools are in the cupboard, have fun." And before the woman could reply, Sally was off and running again.

"Okay, Billy, are you ready for that story now?" she asked, with her son firmly planted in her lap.

"Go for it, mommy."

"Okay, here's a little story I like to call The Wish."

Sally looked down at her son and smiled broadly before she began. "Sally sat at her sewing machine and sighed."

Her son stopped her. "Wait, mommy, does the whole story sound that way? Yuck."

"Well, Billy, here and there. But don't worry; it has a really happy ending. Promise."

Sally smiled and hugged her son good and tight. She had no need for wishes from then on out.

In The Headlights

Jeannie Mobley

As an anthropologist, I know all about witchcraft in traditional cultures. I know about its role in social control, and I know how the power of witchcraft is psychological; for it to work, you have to believe. I have read the studies, analyzed the phenomenon, and explained it in classrooms filled with skeptical students. Still, I wasn't prepared for the truth.

I headed north out of Flagstaff just as the last rays of sun grazed the tips of the San Francisco Peaks and transformed the expanse to the east into a vast haze of russet and purple. The view and the solitude raised my spirits as I broke from the forests and dropped to the desert floor. By the time I turned east onto Highway 160 and cut across the desolate lowland stretch into Tuba City, the landscape was receding into darkness. I cheerfully refilled my tank under the bright florescent lights at a gas station that seemed both too new and too prosperous for that dusty town. I bought a Coke and a candy bar, switched on the headlights, and once again pulled out onto the highway. It was fully dark by the time Tuba City dwindled in my rearview mirror.

No sooner had I returned to the speed limit, then a jackrabbit burst from a tangle of roadside beeweed and onto the highway. It froze in my headlights, looking at me with eyes of helpless bewilderment-- mesmerized by the immensity and the brilliance of the thing that would kill it. I hit the brakes, spraying Coke across the dashboard, but the hapless creature was unavoidable. There was a crack on the bumper, a thump beneath the car, and then the creature was lost in the darkness behind me.

My high spirits quavered. The poor thing, I thought, dying alone and confused, a senseless victim to something from another world, something it could not comprehend. I switched on the radio and allowed the country music and the guttural baritone of the Navajo-language DJ to pull me back to more cheerful thoughts. Soon I was flying along at a comfortably illegal speed, humming a catchy tune and vaguely reflecting on the silly heartbreak in the song. The rabbit was forgotten.

It was on the steady, featureless climb into the slickrock country that everything changed. Suddenly, in the headlights I saw a man crawling across the road on all fours, his lithe, naked body moving with dog-like agility. His skin glistened, drenched with--with what? viscera? blood? afterbirth? He looked like a thing newly born--or newly skinned.

Centered in the orb of my headlights, he looked at me, his eyes reflecting the halogen brightness. He bared his teeth in a feral snarl.

I slammed on the brakes and jerked the steering wheel to the right, careening off the pavement in a spray of gravel. The vehicle came to stop not far off the road, but my headlights angled toward the ditch, illuminating only sagebrush and the enveloping cloud of orange dust my panicked flight had raised. My heart pounded wildly and I stared up at the road, but I could see nothing. Nothing but darkness.

A skinwalker! my adrenaline-drugged brain cried out. A skinwalker--a Navajo witch that could remove his human skin and take on animal form! My heart pounded more wildly, but my logical mind cleared almost immediately in reaction to that wild thought. Don't be a fool, I told myself, no one can do that, witchcraft doesn't work that way. There has to be another explanation. An accident victim--that must be it. The poor man had been hit in the dark. He needed help! I shut my eyes and took a deep breath, trying to calm myself enough to do something. That is when the door latch rattled, and the car jerked violently. I looked through my window into the same face again, the snarl now a hungry grin, the eyes glittering with animal madness as they looked into mine. When his fingers clawed at the door a second time, my foot slammed down on the accelerator.

The car slithered sideways before the wheels caught and propelled me forward through sage and Russian thistle, and finally onto pavement. I fishtailed once, then squealed forward. Directly ahead, a man stood on the road--an average Navajo in blue jeans, flannel shirt, and cowboy boots. He calmly held up a hand to stop me, but I did not stop. There was a crack as he hit the windshield, a thump on the trunk, and then he was lost behind me in the darkness.

I pelted on through the night, my hands white-knuckled on the wheel, my teeth clenched, and my eyes riveted on the empty highway before me. I did not think, I did not even breathe for twenty miles. I saw nothing. The night was now empty. An hour later, as I skimmed between the shadowy hulk of Black Mesa and the moon-washed sweep of Tsegi Canyon, I began to calm down. I slowed the car to something close to the speed limit and began to consider what I had done. I would have to call the police and report it, I couldn't avoid taking responsibility and it would be better to confess than to be hunted down. I would explain to them my panic, the fear for my life. Imagine, a single woman alone on an abandoned stretch of highway, and two men waylaying her--it was self defense!

As my fear eased, it left behind exhaustion. I had planned to continue to Farmington tonight, but now I decided to stop. I was tired, and if I was going to have to face the police, I should do it on The Res, where I hoped they would have some sympathy for my irrational fear of Skinwalkers. I could feel the blood rise to my cheeks as I thought of explaining that one to an Anglo cop.

I slowed again, skulked into the town of Kayenta. I pulled into the first motel I came to, wincing slightly with deja vous as my tires crunched on the gravel driveway. A weathered Navajo in jeans and flannel checked me in and slid the key across the counter to me, and I turned toward the door.

"Hey," he said, and I turned back.

"That your car?" he asked, pointing toward the window with a slight thrust of his chin.

"Yes."

He gave a wrinkled smile, his eyes glittering as

they caught the light of his desk lamp. "Thought so. You cracked your windshield." His voice was soft, but laced with a knowledgeable undertone, as if he was confirming a suspicion, not raising one.

I nodded, speechless. He nodded, too, his smile slipping toward sneer. I backed toward the door. He kept smiling and watching.

Outside, I stood just beyond the circle of light that spilled from the hotel's front window, and I turned back to look at him, trying to ignore the shiver climbing up my spine. He was just disappearing though the back door of the motel office.

I forced myself to turn away, to go to my room, to think clearly. He didn't know--he couldn't! My hand shook as I tried to work the key into the lock. Out of the corner of my eye I saw movement, and I whirled toward it. At the edge of the parkinglot, at the edge of the light, a coyote was watching me, its eyes aglow with reflected brilliance. It licked its lips. As I turned back to the lock, the coyote lifted its head and let out a yipping, mocking howl that pierced the darkness. The key went in, it turned, and the lock released. The coyote's comrades joined him with wild disharmony as I slammed the door behind me, locking, bolting and chaining it as swiftly as I could.

That was a half an hour ago, and that brings me back to this moment--to this knock on the door. I can hear murmured Navajo, feet scuffling, someone breathing. I can hear other noises, too: something sniffing and clawing at my door, and the knob rattling, and turning. The coyotes suddenly sing out in gleeful triumph, and I am realizing something I never told my students. The brotherhood of Skinwalkers is vast, secret, powerful--something from another world, something I cannot comprehend. I am alone and confused, now that I am the one in the headlights.

My Little Elves

Louise Yeiser

When my kids were little, our house was plagued by nocturnal elves whose only goal was to create mischief and cause a stir within our family. I could envision those naughty creatures floating in a corner, up near the ceiling, cross-legged and comfy, whispering together and giggling gleefully at the confusion created in the room below. They were able to witness scenes like this: "William and Eric, who made this mess in the kitchen?" "What mess?" Startled, wide eyes. How could any mother ever have accused either one of these innocent children? "This mess right here. The milk spilled on the counter, the chocolate powder sticking all over the floor, the dirty cup and spoon sitting on the counter that weren't rinsed, so they're all dried up, hard and yucky. That mess!" My hands involuntarily going to my hips, my quit-messing-with-me stance. Eric turning towards William: "Did YOU make chocolate milk last night?" William turning towards Eric: "No. I didn't! Mom, he's trying to get me in trouble!" The ensuing loud argument drifted up, straight to the ears of our little elves, still floating near the ceiling, laughing so hard that they had to cover their mouths with their hands. My lame attempt to intervene and cut to the chase: "Cut it out, you two, and whoever did this, fess up." Those startled, wide eyes again. Oh, brother.

Lord knows, we three could have gone on this way forever. But being the initiator of such an exchange, I often lost interest in pursuing it. It didn't seem worth the trouble. The process required too much patience and energy. Qualities which I needed for other things, such as hunting down misplaced homework, assembling school lunches, catching the dirty clothes before they marched out the door, signing permission slips, checking the school schedule and handling a myriad of other last minute mishaps. I shrugged. "Oh, well, it must have been the elves again."

Those elves! Their mischief fell into two categories: taking and leaving. They liked to take things such as spoons, socks and shoes (only one of a pair), homework, gym shorts, favorite pencils, pens, magic markers, rulers, compasses, hackey sacks, erasers and rocks. The one item they liked to leave was a mess!

With my children grown and gone, it seems that my little elves must have gone with them. My spoons don't magically disappear from my drawers, my socks stay in their proper pairs and those surprise messes haven't appeared in years. Things just aren't the same. I guess there isn't enough for them to do around here anymore. No excitement. No challenge. And I have to admit. Sometimes I miss them.

LEPUS EUROPAEUS

Allan F. Gilbreath

My name is Jack Lago. I'm a detective and I hate holiday crimes. Needless to say, I'm in a real bad mood right now. Lucky me, I pulled graveyard shift for the weekend. The first call came in at two in the morning, a noise complaint. A couple of uniforms checked it out and kicked it up to me. If it gets to me, somebody is dead, literally.

Small snowflakes began sticking to my coat as soon as I got out of the car. These late spring storms drop a little snow at night, but the sun usually wipes it all out by rush hour. I looked at the retail strip center. Nothing looked burned or broken, so I started walking towards the shops. An officer stepped out of a breezeway in the middle of the center and called to me.

"Over here, sir."

I nodded and watched the potentially slick ground as I walked. I don't know why I was looking down so closely. I'm used to walking on winter's little gifts, but the tracks in the snow kept catching my attention. The footprints of the officers and a few other shoe prints going this way and that were expected. What stuck in my mind were the long narrow ones and a few that looked like hoof prints. There's just no telling what you will find in the middle of the night in New Jersey.

"Sir, its back here." The officer urged me down the breezeway to the backside of the center.

"I'm coming," I said as I pulled my camera out of my pocket and snapped a couple of shots.

The alleyway looked like a train wreck. It is a bit shocking to see the commercial dumpsters flipped like wastepaper baskets, trash everywhere. Over against the back fence I could see the area the officers had already taped off. Normally, a crime scene in New Jersey is a flurry of flashing lights, people and noise. This one's distinguishing characteristic, quiet. Quiet always meant murder, a bad one. No murder is good, some are just worse than others. I stepped under the tape and turned to one of the officers.

"What have we got here?"

"I don't really know, sir. This is how we found the scene. We haven't touched a thing." The pasty look on his face told me this wasn't going to be a normal scene.

I took a few more snap shots then put on my evidence gloves. Carefully, I lifted away a battered sheet of cardboard. It's underside covered in blood. Everything underneath it completely soaked in blood. The more trash I moved and photographed, the more blood I found. The one thing I didn't find, a body.

I stood up and looked around the alleyway again. There had been one hell of a fight here and someone obviously didn't make it out alive. The soft snow coated everything and should make the crime scene easy to read. Instead, no drag marks, no blood trail, and the only minimal splatter evidence across the face of the fence. I looked around into the expectant eyes of the two officers standing there watching me.

"Has anyone got a witness statement yet?" I asked the first one.

"No sir, not yet." He pulled his notebook out in anticipation of my next order.

"Okay, you take care of whoever called this in." The first officer began walking away.

I turned to the second officer and said, "Call this in for a complete crime scene work up. I don't want another soul back here trampling the evidence. Got it?"

"Yes sir. Sir, I … " His voice faded out like he was trying to tell me something he didn't want to say.

"What is it?" I looked at his badge and read his name. "Out with it Baker."

"Well, there's one more thing. I was first on the scene. When I walked back here," he paused, "I heard something."

I could see the distress in his eyes. I asked the next question instead of commanding. "Heard what?"

He sighed as if he was putting his career on the line with something wild like a UFO sighting out in the woods. Reports like that stick with you for years and don't let go. "I heard something flapping, like big wings. I don't know how else to describe it."

"Thanks, Baker. I won't put it in unless it means something."

"Thank you sir, let me get this called in." He walked back up the breezeway with the gait of a relived man.

I made my notes and took more shots. I wasn't sure what I was looking for but I learned long ago to record everything and sort it out later. I started to walk back to my car where I could wait somewhere warm. There were those weird footprints again. Now that my eyes were accustom to picking them out, they were everywhere, both kinds. The long ones and the hoof prints seemed to be chasing each other all around the area. The flapping comment stuck in my mind and made me look up into the black sky and listen. All I could hear was the soft hiss of falling snow.

The car heater fought to provide relief from the cold as I collected my notes and thoughts. The real question is how did someone get a bloody corpse out of there without leaving a trail. The first officer I had sent for a statement got back just as crime scene team arrived. I got out of the car just as the heater had made it worthwhile to stay. I walked over to the team leader, Petrofski. She was as good as they came on the topic of how did someone get dead.

"We really got to stop meeting like this." She quipped as I walked over. "People are starting to talk."

"Oh well. Guess what? I got you another holiday special. This is shaping up to go weird on us." I began guiding her down the breezeway. We stopped at the edge of the alleyway. She would want to get her own bearings and I had learned to not interfere with her or her team.

"We got a body over there I suppose?" She asked pointing to the bloody pile of trash.

"That's where we got a body's worth of blood, but no body and no visible exit point." I answered. I looked the scene over one more time, as she looked it over for the first. The odd prints weighed on my mind. "Before your team gets back here, I need you to check something for me."

She looked and me and sighed. "And here comes the weird part, right?"

"Just get me an I.D. on what could make these kinds of marks. Let's just assume some kind of homemade snow gear or something like that." I knelt down and pointed out the odd tracks. She looked them over and nodded.

"Don't worry. I got you covered."

"Thanks. Let me know some results as soon as possible. I want to get this wrapped up before church hits in a few hours." I stood up and stepped back.

"I'll do what I can, Lago."

I walked back up the breezeway to get out of her team's way and find out what the witness had to say. Several people passed me carrying armloads of equipment that would turn that mess back there into evidence I could use. I saw the officer I was looking for. A quick look at his badge got me his name.

"What have you got Owens?"

"The witness lives on the other side of the fence.

She's elderly and lives alone. She woke up to all kinds of animal noises. She got spooked and called it in."

"Animal noises? No voices or anything she could understand?"

"No sir. She said animal noises, like a donkey or horse or something like that." He read his notes carefully.

I hate holiday crimes. They always go weird on you. So, I have a murder scene with lots of blood but no body. Now, I have animal sounds, weird prints and something that flaps. "She see anything?"

"She said that once the noises got started, she called it in and stayed inside."

"At least she had sense enough to stay put and call." I chewed on my bottom lip. This was going to get even more frustrating. I just knew it.

"Umm, sir, there is something in her yard I think you should see." Owens ventured cautiously.

"What is it?" I already had a suspicion what he was going to say.

"There are some kind of prints in the snow across her yard."

"Are they long and narrow or are they like hoof prints?"

Owens, visibly startled by my question, looked around nervously then faced me. His eyes, wide open as he answered. "They are long and narrow. How did you know?"

I smiled at the street hardened but still young face. "Just call it a hunch, Owens. Just call it a hunch."

Owens still had that look on his face when I saw Officer Baker walking over. I figured if this case was going to get weird, I was going to have witnesses. I rubbed my hands together and blew into them in a vain attempt to ward of the cold. It wasn't really that bad. It was just cold enough to be uncomfortable. I gathered my two volunteers or maybe I should say conscripts and we walked around the corner of the block. Just like I expected, there they were, long narrow tracks laid out side by side. I tried to figure out how you could make tracks like that. I didn't like what came to mind.

Baker said it first. "The only way you can make a track like that would to hop."

We all thought it, but I wasn't going to say it out loud. He realized what he said and started shaking his head. He looked up at me and I could almost hear him blaming me for roping him into this. I didn't blame him for the look in his eyes. I had the same look the first case I was on that went weird. Who knows, he might even make detective some day. That is, if he doesn't take early retirement due to mental stress. I think that's what they call going crackers these days.

"Anybody figure out which way this thing came from?" I asked to see if we could find something to do while we waited on the crime scene results. Owens had already started walking across the yard following the trail.

"I think it was going from house to house until it found the gate open here." Owens pointed to the evidence to back up his theory.

I pulled my keys out and tossed them to Baker and told both officers, "Go back and park your cruisers. Bring my car around and call in that the two of you are coming with me. We're going to back track this thing and see where it's been."

They both nodded and walked away. I would have a few minutes alone before they got back, so I kept following the trail. Whoever or whatever made this trail put in a lot of effort. I walked over half the block and the prints were still going. At the end of the block, I stopped and took a deep breath. There was just what I didn't want to see but knew I would find. A trail of hoof print looking tracks crossed the long narrow ones. Did I mention holiday crimes always get weird?

I stood there waiting on the officers to come get

me. I traced the two paths as far as I needed to. If nothing else, this is going to be interesting. As I stood there in the dark and cold, I stamped my feet for warmth and almost missed it. Just at the outside edge of my hearing, something was there. I stood stone still with one hand under my coat on my gun. There it was again, the sound of flapping. I tried as hard as I could to make out where the sound was coming from. I cocked my head from side to side. I got the impression that the sound came from very high overhead but it was getting closer.

The growl of the car engine drowned out the soft winged sound as the officers returned with my car. I motioned for them to kill the engine. Once the car stopped, they both got out and remained silent. The three of us stood there like bizarre yard gnomes each posed for listening. I could see their eyes as they heard the sound. I motioned for them to remain quiet. The flapping appeared to be directly over us and then it moved towards the shopping center. It sounded like it landed.

Baker had been driving so I jumped in the passenger side and Owens just made it into the back seat before we were sliding down the street. Baker killed the lights as we pulled into the parking lot. He patrolled slowly around the perimeter then methodically swept the area in a search pattern. Owens pulled out my spot light and began checking the top of the building. At the far end of the building, we got a shadow. Baker pulled the car out away from the building but angled in so Owens could hit it with the spotlight again. The powerful halogen beam leapt out and reflected back red, two glowing points just above the edge of the building. Whatever it was, we had it on the roof, now what?

We could see the crime team still coming and going from their vehicles. They either thought we were crazy and ignored us or just plain ignored us. Out of the corner of my eye I could see the fire department's paramedic van pulling in. There was no one for them to save but I had a use for that van.

I don't know why I whispered when I spoke but I did. "Baker, run over there and get that meat wagon over here. I got an idea."

He didn't ask any questions or say anything. He didn't have to; the look on his face said it all. He just got slowly out of the car and walked steadily across the parking lot. Steady, unless you count the death lock he had on the grip of his gun. I nodded to Owens and we both got out and watched. The two red points still glowed from the edge of the roof. They moved every so often like glowing eyes watching us and the other activities across the parking lot.

After a couple of minutes, I glanced over and saw Baker headed back with the paramedics. The van rolled slowly to a stop. The driver was looking to see what we had spotlighted.

"You got a small fire hose on that rig, right?" I asked hopefully.

"Yeah. What do you have in mind?" The gum-smacking driver answered.

"Think it will reach up there." I nodded towards the red reflections.

He looked up, smacked his gum a couple more times then finally said, "It should hit it pretty good."

Owens, you keep the light on that thing. Baker, take this camera and get a picture of this idiot when we get him to stand up." I tossed him a disposable camera and continued. "If some fool hang glides in on a roof at night, we'll just get his wings wet and see if he wants to fly off of there."

The paramedics rolled out the sprayer and adjusted the nozzle for spray, not the normal setting for mist. Everyone looked ready.

"Hit it."

The water arched up the side of the building then right on the glowing red spots. They went out. We kept the water going for a moment more when something screamed. It sounded like a cross between a mule braying and fingernails on a chalkboard. I'm not sure what happened next but I saw the camera go off and something sail off that roof right at us. Water went everywhere. There was something in the middle of it all. It looked like a starved horse with very short front legs, long back legs and huge bat wings. We all hit the deck. It swooped over us and disappeared into the night.

After we all got done cussing and exclaiming, I retrieved my camera and we calmed the paramedics down. There for a couple of minutes, I thought we were going to have to call for more paramedics to take care of our first ones. Eventually, we got it all settled down and finished up the crime scene.

It was dawn, so I decided to head into the station to figure this mess out and wait for the crime scene reports. Owens and Baker both brought me their reports. They did as good a job as they could under the circumstances. They both had that "UFO in the woods" look on their faces. I was afraid they were right. I sent the camera down for developing. It was just a matter of time now, or so I thought.

With the sunrise came the calls, hundreds of them. People all over the area reported strange prints in the snow. There were prints on walls, trees, rooftops, sidewalks, and fences. It was like these things had literally run all over town until they met up behind the strip center. We literally had every available officer out taking reports and doing their best to control the rumors that were already flying. The sun managed to warm things up enough by Easter Service to erase the snow and the enigmatic prints. There were a few trapped in mud puddles. We managed to take some very poor quality plaster casts before the mud dried out and the tracks disappeared.

The combination of church and sunshine got everyone's mind off the odd prints and the day looked like it was going to settle down. I sat down behind my desk and leaned back until my chair creaked in protest. My mind ran over the events of the past few hours. Nothing really made sense, at least not yet. Hopefully, the crime scene reports and, if I got real lucky, a photograph or two would clear all this up.

Owens and Baker were the first ones in from the streets with the plaster casts. I could read the look in their eyes as they walked up to my desk. They had the look of men condemned to working with me on every crackpot case that comes in from now on. They looked like they were bringing me the proverbial UFO from the woods.

"What have we got guys." I figured I would start this morbid little party right. Baker just shook his head from side to side and looked up at Owens.

"We took the casts. I'm not sure about them." Owens set them carefully on the desk as if they were snaked he didn't want to wake.

"Baker, get me a sand box and let's see what we got here." I said as I began unfolding the crumpled newspaper. There they were, dirty plaster casts with one set in the shape of a hoof, the other set was long and narrow with some kind of little bumps at one end. I held each up in turn. Casts are actually the negatives to the footprints. Sometimes, pressing them into clean moist sand can give you better idea of what you are looking at that than what you saw at a crime scene. I could see Baker coming back with his hands full. I shoved a few things aside to make room.

"Just set it here." I pointed to the clear spot.

He set the box down and opened the lid. Owens took the little smoothing tool to the surface of the sand a couple of times to make sure there were no stray marks to fool us later. I looked the hoof prints over and held them for everyone to see.

"Let's try these first." I announced and looked as

every one nodded in agreement. Carefully, I laid them out on the sand then pressed them in. We waited just a moment to make sure the imprint took. As I lifted the casts I said, "Here goes nothing."

Everyone held their breath as I pulled the casts away. We all stared for a full minute. I don't know what we expected to find but when you press hoof print shaped casts in to sand, guess what, you get hoof prints. In this case, they looked like the hoof prints of an unshod pony. We all looked at the prints then looked at each other. Three pairs of eyes all looked back at the prints and then met in the middle again.

Baker took a deep breath and shrugged. He shook his head and said, "Well, I guess this means the chemical plant down by the river gets to explain a flying pony that runs up walls and eats people."

Owens and I just looked at him. He smiled at us and continued, "Hey, it makes about as much sense as anything else we've seen."

He had us there. What brilliant thing was I going to deduce that sounded any less outlandish? I decided that ducking the issue was the best way to go at this point.

"Okay guys," I sighed. "Go home and get some rest. I'll let you know what we get from Petrofski's report."

They looked relived as they got away from the sand box and my desk. I was happy they were ready to go because I wanted to try the long tracks and I had a suspicion they really didn't want to know. I smoothed the sand and carefully placed the casts in the box. I pressed them in deeply and hesitated before I lifted them. I set my teeth firmly together as if this were a weight lifting exercise and lifted the casts out. I stared at the prints for a while. The odd bumps at the front of the cast made little claw like marks at the end of a long narrow foot. A childhood memory of trying to catch a cottontail came to mind. I remembered seeing a track like this back then. The only difference would be scale. This rabbit would have been an elephant among rabbits and we never saw any front prints. A flying pony and now a giant walking rabbit. I erased the sand and sat down heavily into my complaining chair.

I closed my eyes and began working up the "official" story. This process is sort of like taking a bite out of an exotic meal then making up the recipe and how it was cooked. It doesn't matter if you are vaguely close to the truth. All that matters is the story covers the basic points.

" Lepus europaeus."

The words were accompanied by a thump of a report folder landing on my desk. Petrofski's voice had the sound of a mother demanding to know why she found a frog in the refrigerator. I opened my eyes and spun my chair around to face her.

"Leapy what?" I had to ask.

" Lepus europaeus is what the blood and hair analysis came back with. You want to tell me what the hell is going on here?" Petrofski didn't look amused as she waited for an answer.

"What is a lepus eurowhatsit?" My look of ignorance was quite sincere. I didn't have a clue what she was talking about.

She gave me a condescending look then took the attitude that she was about to be one up on me. She answered, " Lepus europaeus is the Latin name for the common European brown hare. What are we doing with a crime scene, European rabbit fur and enough rabbit blood for a couple dozen bunnies?"

One thing leapt to my mind, she had not seen the thing on the roof. I had one way out of explaining killer flying ponies so I took it. I said, "I am not so sure we actually have a crime scene per say."

"What do you mean?" She was waiting for more.

I scrambled mentally to my tiptoes. "What I mean is, someone may have been butchering their rabbits back there. That would explain the fur and the blood and maybe even the noise our elderly witness called in."

"If that's the case, then we are out of it. This sounds more like a case for the health department or possibly an animal cruelty case if we ever find out what happened to the rabbits." Petrofski sounded like I was going to get away with it until she continued. "So what about those weird tracks all over the place?"

I still had one more good dance step left in me. "I am going to go over those with the meteorological guys and see if those weren't the work of something freaky about the snow this late in the year.

Petrofski just shrugged and pushed the papers closer to me and said, "Well, just let me know how you want to close this one out." She turned and started to walk off. She called back over her shoulder, "I got more work to get done, oh let me know what really happened some day."

Okay, so I didn't get away clean, but I got away clean on paper and that's all that really counts anyway. I was still going to check with one more person before I gave up on this one. Everyone knows someone that seems to know just a little too much about UFO's, Bigfoot, sea monsters, and the tooth fairy. I bundled up the files, casts, and everything else connected with this case headed for the photo lab. I signed for my pictures, stuffed them in my coat pocket and made it to my car without having to answer any more questions.

As I drove, I tried to collect my thoughts. How was I going to approach this? I came up with several clever ploys. I picked the best couple as I pulled in the driveway. Good his car was here. Hollis Ickerson knew everything there was too know about any obscure topic you could think of and I was going to put him to the test. I carried my armload of stuff up to his door and knocked. Hollis answered and all my great thoughts abandoned me and my cleverest ploy was to hand him the armload and say, "What do you make of all this?

Two hours I sat there while Hollis dug through the evidence. I was ready to start chewing the wallpaper. He just kept looking through the stuff again and again. The occasional hmmm or headshake was all I got. I finally remembered the photos and pulled them out of my pocket and flipped through them. I felt a cold chill run down my spine as I looked at the last picture. There that thing was. It was right there on film. We really had seen the thing. Hollis noticed the look on my face.

"What have you got there?" He asked expectantly.

"Alright, you tell me what you think, then I'll show you the picture." I had to know if he came up with the same idiot answer that was sitting in my brain.

Hollis cleared his throat and began, "You know how Halloween is supposed to be the night the spirit world can come out to play and full moons are supposed to make people act funny?"

"Yeah." I looked him in the eye. "That's what the costumes are all about right? "Trust me, you learn all about full moons when you're a cop."

"Okay, let's just assume that Halloween is not the only time things can get an little supernatural."

I nodded. "Sounds fair enough."

"And that the New Jersey Pine Barrens have their own legend." He prompted.

"We got the Jersey Devil or something like that."

"Exactly." Hollis looked at me like I was about to get a gold star. He raised his eyebrows expectantly and waited for me to make a few connections.

I tried to wait him out but the thoughts were already running amok. I leaned back and rubbed my face with both hands. "So, you are trying to tell me that Easter is kinda like Halloween in the fact that things could get a little supernatural and that this means the Jersey Devil could get out and go running around."

"Exactly." Hollis absolutely beamed. I just felt like an idiot with a new village. Hollis continued, "Do you remember that movie with the giant invisible rabbit?"

"Ummm, the one that hung out in bars and insane asylums?" I had the feeling that the mental version of a train wreck was about to happen.

"That's the one." He affirmed. It scared me to think Hollis was getting into all this and still smiling. He had that lecture look in his eye again. "It was a pooka, which is described in the movie as, "From old Celtic mythology, a fairy spirit in animal form, always very large. It is a benign but mischievous creature.""

"Wait, wait, wait." My brain just took a hard left and I think the rest of me slid into the passenger seat. "You're trying to tell me that one of those things got loose too and then got the stuffing kicked out of it."

Hollis smiled as he leaned back in his chair and smugly said, "If you have better theory, I would love to hear it. Quid pro quo?"

"Squid what?"

Hollis looked annoyed then said, "Lets see this picture. I told you what I think. Let's have it."

I put my precious picture in his hand. He looked at it very closely for several minutes. He finally handed it back to me and said, "Welcome to the club."

"What club?"

"The "I think I saw something - check out my blurry picture" club." Hollis said with practiced ease. "The same club millions of people are in. We see something strange, we get the best evidence we can and it still won't be enough. Even if you dropped a body on the desk, the world still won't believe you because it messes with the "normal" way of thinking of the world."

I looked at the picture again. Sure enough, my memory was filling in the blurred parts. You could almost make out what it was but not quite. It had just been moving too fast. I thanked him for his help and loaded all my junk back into the car, after promising Hollis he could have the casts when I was done with them. Now that I had enough information to make a somewhat rational report, I think I will stick with somebody getting a few rabbits ready for the stew pot and freaky weather. There is no way I am going to turn in a report that says the Jersey Devil ate the Easter Bunny.

In The Name of Desdemonia

Nicholas Knight

They're all scum! Men! Each and every one of them…scum!

Shar had hoped that coming to her favorite spot in the woods would calm her down, but being alone with her thoughts only served to heighten her bitterness. The peaceful green pond, the charming symphony of birds and insects — none of it cheered her up.

It had been less than an hour since she'd been dumped for the umpteenth time. Grayden had the "courtesy" to wait until after the graduation ceremonies were over to tell her that he'd accepted a job in Denver — and that he wanted to go alone. Did he care that Shar had accepted a job in Wyoming because that's where they'd planned on settling down and starting a family? No, of course not, because he was a man!

As she sat on her favorite rock, still wearing her cap and gown, she wondered where her life was going and if she could ever trust another man again. Tears rolled freely down her face, salt intertwined with streaks of green and black makeup. A ladybug landed on her nose, causing her to giggle. But the smiles were unwelcome, so she blew upward in an attempt to dislodge the tickling insect. The ladybug fluttered its wings, but kept its perch. Frustrated, she blew harder, sending the little creature spinning towards the pond.

Feeling momentarily guilty, Shar felt relieved when the ladybug regained its equilibrium, just short of plunging into the depths of the algae-encrusted pond. Absentmindedly, she followed the insect's flight for a few seconds, until it disappeared behind an ugly frog. Actually, Shar was pretty sure that the ladybug had disappeared into the frog's mouth, but she preferred not to think of it that way.

Strangely enough, the frog seemed to be staring at her. She tried to shrug it off and look away, but she couldn't shake the feeling. Shar nearly cried out in surprise when the frog hopped out of the pond and onto a rock less than a foot in front of her.

She leaned forward to get a better look at the warty amphibian. Wouldn't it be nice if the fairy tales were true and this frog was actually a dashing prince? A prince that would be forever in her debt if she changed him back into a man.

"What the hell — you only live once," she muttered, as she leaned closer to the frog. She puckered up, then lost her nerve and jerked away.

She searched her pockets and found a mint, figuring it wouldn't kill her to kiss the thing so long as she had something to rid her mouth of the awful taste she expected to encounter. Not wanting to think anymore, just wanting to act, she quickly leaned forward, closed her eyes, and planted her lips on the frog's mouth.

At first cold and rubbery, the frog's lips seemed to turn warm and soft, much like a human's. Shar became lost in the moment, imagining herself kissing a handsome prince. She was almost enjoying herself — it felt so real!

Shar felt a long, hot tongue probing the inside of her mouth.

Startled, she opened her eyes, and nearly gagged. Instead, she fell backwards screaming.

She'd been kissing an old woman! The most hideous woman she'd ever seen. "Hag" was the word that came to mind. Shar closed her eyes again, wishing the woman away. But when she re-opened them, the hag was still there — and she was smiling.

"Ribbit." The old hag looked confused by her own voice. She cleared her throat for what seemed like an eternity to the horrified Shar, then tried again. "Thank you, my child, for setting me free."

"Wh-wh-who are you?" Shar managed to ask.

"I've been known by many names, but after being trapped in a frog's body for so long, I think it only fitting I start fresh with a new name. And in honor of your wonderful deed, you can call me 'Freeda!'"

Relaxing slightly, Shar summoned the courage to ask Freeda how she'd been turned into a frog.

Freeda scowled angrily. "A jealous, jealous witch put a spell on me."

Shar was about to ask her if she used the term "witch" literally, but reconsidered, assuming the answer to be yes in light of the transformation she'd just witnessed. Instead, she asked Freeda if she, herself, was a witch. Shar hated to make stereotypes, having been the victim of them often enough herself. Freeda looked so much like a story-book witch, right down to the wart on the end of her nose — though she supposed the blemish could have been a lingering effect of the frog spell.

Freeda chuckled — rather, cackled — amusedly. "Indeed I am, child, indeed I am." And as if to demonstrate, she waved her hand and was suddenly clothed all in black, with a pointed black hat.

Shar couldn't help but snicker.

"What's so funny, girl?" Freeda asked, looking irritated.

"I'm sorry, it's just that I didn't think that witches actually dressed like that…"

"Of course we do. But only on special occasions and wouldn't you agree that this is a special occasion?"

"Yes, of course. I'm sorry."

"That's all right. There wouldn't be anything for me to celebrate if it wasn't for you. In fact, I think that you deserve a reward for setting me free!"

"Is this where you grant me three wishes?" Shar joked.

"I said I was a witch, not some ridiculous genie in a bottle!" Freeda nearly shouted.

Sensing that she had somehow touched a nerve, Shar began to apologize, but was cut off.

"Actually," the witch said thoughtfully, "why

not? I will grant you three wishes — no, five wishes!"

"Really?" Shar couldn't believe her luck.

"Yes. And I won't impose any silly restrictions on you either. If you want to wish for someone to fall madly in love with you, then go ahead…I can make it happen. If you want someone dead…" the witch smiled cruelly, "then wish it and they will die."

A chill ran down Shar's spine.

"But," Freeda continued, "don't go getting any ideas about wishing for more wishes. That will only annoy me, and you don't want to annoy me."

Suddenly the sky turned dark, and threatening clouds rumbled overhead. Shar shivered uneasily. No, she definitely did not want to annoy this witch.

It occurred to Shar that she might waste her wishes accidentally, so she asked Freeda how exactly the whole wish-granting thing would work.

"You are a bright girl. I will make it so that the wishes only work when you say, 'In the name of Desdemonia, I wish for…'"

"Desdemonia? Not Freeda?"

"That is the name that will be recognized by the Powers from Beyond — so choose your wishes wisely.

"Now," the witch said abruptly, "it is time for me to depart. I have a wish of my own to fulfill." There was a blinding flash of light and the witch was gone, the dark clouds disappearing with her.

~~~~~

Shar returned to her apartment in a daze. Had she really just turned a frog into a witch? Would she really be able to have her wildest dreams come true?

She entered her apartment to find a familiar leather jacket draped over the back of the couch — Grayden's leather jacket. Shar was filled with a mix of hope and dread, wondering why he was here. She even contemplated wishing for him to fall in love with her.

Not seeing him, she headed for her bedroom expecting to find him there. Instead, he rushed out of her roommate's bedroom. At first Shar was too confused to notice that he was barely dressed, but seeing her half-naked roommate dressing hurriedly in the background made everything all too clear.

"Shar — I can explain," Grayden said awkwardly. "I came by to say goodbye to you, and…"
~~~~~

"And you said 'Hello' to Angela instead!" Shar cut in angrily.

"I didn't expect to ever see you again…"

"Just get out!"

"Come on Shar — no hard feelings, okay?"

"Yeah, right," Shar replied, on the verge of tears. "I wish you were dead!"

Grayden gasped, held his hand to his chest, and staggered around in great pain.

Shar was horrified. Oh no! What have I done?

"That hurts, Shar — that really hurts," Grayden lamented.

Realizing that he'd just been putting on an act, Shar's anger returned and for an instant she contemplated actually saying the proper words: "In the name of Desdemonia, I wish…"

Seeing that his performance hadn't softened Shar's mood, Grayden reached for his jacket. "Well, whatever," he said, heading for the door. "I'm outta here. Have a nice life."

The door slammed, and for a moment Shar just stared blankly at the spot where Grayden had just been. Then she ran into her own room, and slammed the door behind her — she wasn't in any mood to deal with Angela.

For a while, she just laid on her bed, crying quietly. Eventually, her self-pity was replaced by anger, which rapidly escalated into pure rage. She'd never felt this way before, yet she found herself welcoming the dark emotion. The rage that coursed through her veins coupled with the power that she knew she held over the world — thanks to the witch's wishes.

Shar became blinded to all reason. She just longed to hurt those who'd hurt her.

Make a wish!

Her pain took on its own voice, whispering seductively, urgently…

Make them pay!

Shar found herself speaking, as if in a trance, "In the name of Desdemonia, I wish that Grayden Toff…"

…was dead!

Shar couldn't bring herself to finish the wish. It was a struggle. The desire within her was great. Still, she was a good person at the core, so was unable to wish real harm upon her betrayers. Instead, she wished bad luck upon them.

"In the name of Desdemonia, I wish for Grayden Toff's job in Denver to fall through!"

Shar could feel the power of the wish; there

was electricity in the air. She hungered for more.

"In the name of Desdemonia, I wish for Angela Sind to become…uh, become…fat and ugly!"

The level of electrical energy rose, causing Shar's skin to tingle ecstatically. There was an audible "pop" and then it was over. Everything became still and quiet.

"AAAAAUGHHHHH!"

A shriek from Angela's room broke the fragile silence. "Shar! Help meeeeee!"

Shar rushed into the living room, and nearly crashed into Angela. At least, she thought it was Angela. The girl standing in front of her only bore a slight resemblance to her roommate. She was now a much fatter, uglier Angela.

"What is happening to me?" the grotesque girl wailed.

Shar looked on in horror as Angela's clothes ripped open and tore off, her skin stretched impossibly tight over her expanding mass.

Angela screamed in pure agony as her skin split open all over her body. The scream strained the corners of her mouth; the skin cracked open and jagged gashes extended rapidly across her pockmarked cheeks.

A disgusting gurgling drew Shar's attention to

Angela's enormous stomach, which seemed to be pulsing in an erratic pattern. With each pulse, something bulged forth from within the massive belly, something that longed to break free of its gelatinous tomb.

Shar took a terrified step backwards as she realized that there were hands pushing against her friend's skin. She gasped as the outline of a face pressed savagely against it. It was Freeda's face!

Freeda's hideous visage stretched forward, between two claw-like hands that reached out to Shar. Shar backed away, but tripped over an ottoman and crashed to the ground, still facing the gruesome scene.

Angela's stomach exploded, pelting Shar with bloody chunks of flesh and shredded intestines. Shar's own stomach convulsed, and she vomited onto her chest.

What have I done? Shar thought to herself, as she wiped remnants of the bile from around her mouth. Slowly, she looked up at her roommate who was still alive, but had a big gaping hole in her midsection. Angela's puffy face was caked in blood and she seemed unable to talk; her lips had disappeared amidst her ever-expanding cheeks. Her eyes seemed glossy, but Shar could see that they were begging for mercy. Shar felt disgusted with herself for letting her rage consume her senses and was suddenly determined to make amends. "In the name of Desdemonia, I wish that my last…"

No wait! Not just my last wish! Images of Grayden working at his new job and mysteriously falling through the floor of a high-rise building to his death fifty stories below flashed urgently through her mind.

"In the name of Desdemonia, I wish that my last two wishes be reversed!"

Without realizing it, Shar had clenched her eyes tightly shut. Slowly, she opened them. Angela stood above her, and other than having a confused expression on her face, she looked perfectly normal. Shar was so overwhelmed with relief that she nearly vomited again.

"What just happened?" Angela asked timidly.

"I…I…I think you were having a nightmare. I heard you screaming and I rushed out here to find you sleepwalking. I must have woke you up when I tripped over the ottoman."

Angela didn't appear to believe Shar's explanation, but it was obvious that she desperately wanted to. She opened her mouth, and then closed it again without saying a word.

Shar just shrugged her shoulders, and rushed back to her bedroom. As she shut the door behind her, she saw Freeda's ugly mug laughing at her through the mirror hanging on her door. Shar yelled at her to leave her alone and smashed her fist into the glass to eliminate the repulsive image. She failed. The mirror broke into a million tiny shards. Each piece continued to reflect Freeda's hideous face, only now she seemed to be laughing at her even harder. Shar was not about to give her any more satisfaction. She wrapped a towel around her bloody hand, and buried herself under her covers. The broken glass and her remaining wishes would just have to wait until tomorrow.

~~~~~

Shar spent most of the night tossing and turning as she tried to figure out how she could use her last two wishes safely. She dejectedly contemplated whether she should even use them at all.

When sleep finally came to her, it was a restless, troubled sleep. She dreamt that Freeda was hovering over her bed, chanting evil spells. She dreamt that the reversal wish had caused Angela to become thinner and prettier until she shriveled up and turned to
~~~~~

dust. And she had darker, more disturbing dreams of demons digging their claws into her body, trying to rip her soul out.

~~~~~

Shar woke up with the sun, unable to fall back to sleep. She took a long, hot shower, but it did little to lift her fatigue. While in the shower, she contemplated her next wish. She resolved that, for better or worse, she would use her last two wishes immediately. She dressed hurriedly, then laid on her bed to summon her courage.

"In the name of Desdemonia, I wish that I had a million dollars!"

A surge of pure energy swirled around her, forcing her to close her eyes for fear of being blinded. Suddenly, her nose was assaulted, as a strong reek of decay threatened to overwhelm her. It reminded her of the time she'd found a dead, rotting mouse behind her fridge, only this stench was a lot more putrid, and closer. Judging by the squishy, sticky surface that she was running her hands over, Shar was fairly certain that she was now lying on the source of the disgusting odor.

Shar willed her eyes open, only to find that she
~~~~~

still couldn't see anything. She reached her hands around, searching for a light-switch or something. To her great dismay, she discovered that she was stuck in a very confined space. There were no latches or doorknobs to be found, nor was she able to move the nearby walls or ceiling no matter how hard she pushed.

The interior of the enclosure felt like satin, and the roof seemed thin somehow. Shar raked her fingers along the material. It ripped open, and the stuffing came tumbling down on her. Only, it wasn't like any stuffing she'd ever felt before; this stuff was like money, bundles of money.

Shar didn't have to see or count the cash to know how much was there. There was no doubt in her mind that there was exactly one million dollars in the tight space with her.

"Damn you Freeda!" she moaned, realizing that she probably wouldn't be able to actually spend the money. In fact, Shar was finally grasping the graveness of her situation. The dark sealed quarters, the decomposing body...

She was in a coffin, at least six feet below the ground.

"I've heard of people wanting to be buried with their riches, but what kind of freak actually does it?" Shar griped, trying to make light of the situation to help keep her wits about her. But the terror in her voice belied her levity, she was on the verge of panic.

Shar was having trouble breathing. There was very little air in her tomb. She struggled to find a way out — pushing and scratching hysterically at the casket to no avail.

"I'm going to die!"

Her first instinct was to reverse her last wish.

"In the name of Desdemonia, I wish—" Shar's voice faltered. Her lungs felt as though they were on fire, and the pain was almost unbearable, but that was not what caused her hesitation. She wondered if she was already too far gone, and questioned if she could trust Desdemonia to actually heal her properly. What if she came back to life as a brain-eating zombie? What if her body still died, and her soul was trapped for all eternity in a slowly rotting animated corpse?

"Damn you Freeda!"

The pain began to fade, and she could feel herself passing in and out of consciousness. It's now or never. Shar knew what she had to do.

With her last breath, she uttered her final wish.

"In the name of Desdemonia, I wish for Freeda

— Desdemonia, whoever the hell she is — to spend all eternity as a frog!"

RULES OF MAGIC

Helen Grant

I've always hated weddings, and my brother's did nothing to reconcile me to the idea. A marriage is supposed to be made in Heaven, and the big day itself is supposed to be "magical". Whoever first applied that epithet to a wedding either knew very little about magic – real magic, I mean, not the fairytale sort – or else he had a very jaundiced view of the future of that particular union. And yet – in some ways a marriage is a little like magic: it giveth, but it also taketh away. Think about it: you gain Love, and you lose Independence. You gain Fidelity, but you lose Excitement. So it is with magic. You've heard all the old tales, of course: the old man who wishes for gold on a withered monkey's paw, and gets it in exchange for his only son's death. The youth who wishes that his portrait would age instead of himself, and loses his soul in the bargain. Did you think these were just stories?

It goes back as far as mankind itself, you know:

indeed, somewhere in modern Greece to this very day and hour there is a tiny wrinkled chirping thing, aged beyond belief, so senile that it has forgotten its own name: Tithonus, who rashly wished for eternal life without wishing for eternal youth, and became so shrunken and scrawny that he turned into a grasshopper. That's the thing about magic – you have to look out for the catch. If there weren't a catch – well, by now all the wealth and power of the world would be concentrated in the hands of a few adepts, wouldn't it? The fact is that you can fairly safely wish for something small: the return of a lost item, perhaps, or the cure of a minor ailment. But try to get into the big time and your way is beset with pitfalls. Would you really wish an errant lover back if he or she were afflicted with a horrible and highly infectious disease? Would you wish for great wealth if it came to you in a way that would forever alienate you from the society of every decent person – including those you love? Maybe you wouldn't – but then again, maybe you would. Many have made that decision, many more than you would imagine. But there is one thing that you should never wish for through magic – and that is a child.

But returning to the subject of my brother's wedding – well, I wouldn't have gone to it at all if my mother hadn't begged me to. I'd had the invitation a month before, had read it with a sort of horrid fascination, and then I'd forgotten about it. Well, perhaps forgotten isn't quite the right word; ignored might be nearer the mark. But either way I hadn't done anything about it. When my mother telephoned, I was sitting in my grandfather's old captain's chair by the window, gazing out over the rooftops at the pale sky. A blackbird flew down and landed on the outside sill. We were regarding each other with friendly disinterest when the telephone rang.

"P —" said my mother, using the name I was given at birth, a name I no longer answer to. "It's me, Mother. Don't hang up."

"I wasn't going to," I said. I've never quarrelled with my mother — not unless you consider that quarrelling with her husband — my father — automatically constitutes bad blood between us. "How are you, Mother?" I asked her.

She sounded impatient. "I'm well. Did you get the invitation?"

"What invitation?" I said, then: "You mean the white lacy one with the cherubs on it?"

"Your brother's wedding invitation," she said, with a you-know-perfectly-well-what-I-mean tone of voice.

"Yes, I did."

"You haven't replied," she said.

I considered telling her that I hate weddings, that I particularly hate weddings which feature white lace and cherubs, that I had no intention of exposing myself either to the cherubs or to the disapproval of the majority of our large extended family. However, in the end all I said was, "I thought it was a gesture. I didn't think I was actually expected to attend."

"Well, you are," she said, and I could hear the strain in her voice. "I – we – really would like you to be there…Purslane."

I could tell that using that name required an effort on her behalf. And I wasn't fooled by that we. It was my mother who wanted me there. My father would have preferred me to stay as far away as possible. My brother holds similar views to my father's, and although he is not quite in the thou-shalt-not-suffer-a-witch-to-live league, I doubted very much that he would welcome me at his wedding either. Poor Mother; always trying to hold the family together; it is a task reminiscent of those set to some hapless heroine in a fairy tale – emptying a well with a sieve, or spinning straw into gold. In ordinary parlance: it isn't going to work.

In the end, though, I let her talk me round. Why

not go? I thought. It was not as though I had anything else planned. Not for the daytime, anyway; I rarely do. And it might even be entertaining, seeing their faces, all of them, the fussy cousins, the prim aunties. Great-Aunt Marjorie in particular, my mother's aunt: she always did look as though she had taken a swig of neat lemon juice whenever she saw me. This time perhaps that weasel mouth of hers would implode completely. My mother, however, knows me well – perhaps too well - and once she had received my assurances that I would be at the cherub-infested wedding, she followed it up with: "And Purslane, please – don't wear black." Having summarily excluded ninety per cent of my wardrobe, she rang off, satisfied.

I think I take after my mother's side of the family – in looks I certainly do. My mother is petite, dark-haired and dark-eyed, light-boned. When she stands next to my father she looks like a willow sapling struggling to grow in the shadow of an oak tree. I inherited my stubborn streak from my father, much though it pains me to admit that I inherited anything from his side of the family; but what Great-Aunt Marjorie disapprovingly calls my "fey side" definitely came from my mother. My maternal grandmother, whisperingly described as eccentric by the rest of the family, was only kept in tolerable order by dint of marriage to a much older, iron-willed man of the cloth, thus setting the pattern for her own daughter's life. Perhaps you are beginning to understand my distaste for the celebration of matrimony? Still, in deference to my mother's wishes I didn't go to my brother's wedding in black, appropriate though it might have been: I chose lavender and purple, a kind of half-mourning. Even Great-Aunt Marjorie couldn't find fault with those colours. I selected a pale lavender silk blouse, a Victorian one which I had picked up for a song from a second-hand shop, because it was too tiny for anyone else to squeeze their twenty-first century frame into. The lavender silk was overlaid with a fine tracery of black lace. I fastened the collar with a tiny cameo surrounded by winking hematite. I chose an ankle-length skirt of deep purple taffeta shot through with a lighter shade which silvered the cloth like a water-mark, and a pair of the highest and spikiest heels I could find. I did not intend that the aunts should look down on me physically at any rate. Then I was ready. I never carry a bag, and I had sent the wedding gift on ahead.

I do have a certain affection for my brother, in spite of the physical and behavioural similarity he bears to my father. Having no wish to disrupt his wedding ceremony with the exclamations of outraged maiden aunts and straight-laced cousins, I did not make a grand entrance of any sort, but slipped into the church when nearly everyone else was already inside, and slid into a pew at the back. This did not prevent several of them (who had heard the tell-tale click of disgracefully high heels on the tiled floor) from turning around in their pews and giving me the sort of looks which curdle milk and make livestock spontaneously abort. Thankfully the thrilling sound of the wedding march striking up distracted them, and I was able to sit peacefully behind a pillar and watch the proceedings undisturbed.

It was the first time I had seen my brother's fiancée; indeed I had not seen my brother himself for over two years. He had put on weight, I noticed when I saw him standing expectantly at the altar, smiling at his bride-to-be as she wafted up the aisle on the arm of her father. I could not see very much of her at all under the voluminous veil which floated around her. Even when she put it back, she had her back to me, and all I could see was a confection of lustrous blonde hair. I had a good look during the recessional though, and I have to say she really did look like a fairytale princess. Briar Rose, perhaps

– not one of the really bright ones. But stunning nevertheless. After the ceremony, when everyone was milling around on the hotel lawn clutching glasses of champagne, I spoke to her very briefly. I went up to her and put out my hand. "Congratulations," I said very gravely. My brother, who had been talking to someone over his shoulder, looked round and said, "Oh," then, "Sam, this is my sister, P –" – he was about to say that birth name I hate, but then he hastily changed it to

"– Purslane."

"Purslane…?" She looked at me curiously, a little furrow marring her otherwise perfect brows. "Was it you that sent us the –?"

"Yes," my brother cut in.

She frowned. "It was very…well, we weren't sure whether we were supposed to…" Her voice trailed off. "Thank you, anyway." She looked up at my brother, then back at me, and gave an embarrassed little smile.

"Thank you, too," I said, and then, since I couldn't think of anything else to say, I walked away.

My brother enjoyed seven months of married bliss before a van driver going too fast for the rainy conditions took it all away, with one smooth skid that catapulted him straight into the afterlife and left my brother to limp on for ten days on a life-support machine. I visited him once, in the evening when everyone else had gone home, exhausted, to eat. I held his limp hand, the knuckles covered in grazes that would never have time to heal over. I had wondered – you know. But his time was up, and I know better than to meddle with Death's schedule. I tried to find one square inch of unbandaged forehead to plant a cold kiss on, and then I left without looking back.

A week later Samantha came to see me.

I was sitting by the window again, staring up at the endless expanse of sky, when the door-bell rang. By the time I had clattered down the three flights of stairs to the street door, it was ringing again, insistently. I opened the door and someone almost fell into the hallway. It was Samantha; Sam, as my brother liked to call her. I regarded her with foreboding: the recently-bereaved are like gelignite, dangerous to handle, and grief was boiling off Sam in waves. She didn't bother with any of the usual social niceties; she stumbled into my house and said, "You've got to help me."

It took some little effort to persuade her to come upstairs to the kitchen and sit down before she told me what she wanted. She would have blurted the whole story out in the hallway. I made her a warming drink, which she regarded with suspicion.

"What is it?"

"It's tea – fruit tea," I said truthfully. "Cherry, if you must know."

"Oh," she said, looking a little ashamed. Then: "Purslane, you've got to help me."

"I'm very sorry, Sam," I said, sliding into the chair opposite her. I reached across the table and clasped her hand. "I truly am. But…"

She cut right through what I was about to say. "I know Robert's gone." Tears were welling up in her cornflower-blue eyes, I noticed with alarm. "I know you can't change that. But you can still help me."

I let go of her hand. "I don't understand what you mean."

"You do, you do." The tears were running freely now, smudging the perfect make-up. "Robert told me – he told me what you are."

He did, did he? "No," I said, shaking my head.

"You have to help me," she said, her voice rising to a wail.

"I'm sorry."

"You have to," she said again, but this time her voice was lower, almost a growl. The bright blonde hair was dishevelled now and she glared at me through a cage of strands, like a wild animal at bay.

This time I didn't even bother to contradict her. I got to my feet.

"I'll tell them," she said, suddenly. I paused for a moment, and in that moment she knew she had me. Her eyes became diamond-bright.

"Tell them what?" I said as casually as I could, but it was too late.

"Robert told me," she said, sniffling. She wiped her nose with the back of her hand. "About Andrew. About the mandrake root."

I stared at her for a long time. "It was justice," I said in the end.

"He was your father's brother," she replied. She was dry-eyed now, watching me. "Your parents don't ever have to know. You just have to help me with this one thing."

I sighed very heavily. Why is it always just this one little thing? "What are you asking me to do?"

"I want Robert's baby," she said. I opened my mouth to say something, but she cut across me again. "I know Robert's gone. I can cope with that – if I have his baby." She stared at me defiantly. "I know you can help me, Purslane, because you're a w-"

This time I cut her off. I can't bear to hear that

word.

"Are you pregnant?" My voice was unintentionally hard.

"No," she said, shaking her head.

"Are you sure?"

"Yes." She nodded. "There's no way."

"Then better you forget the whole idea," I told her. "You don't know what you're asking."

"I don't care. I want a baby," she insisted. Her fists were clenched on the table top, her eyes fierce. "I want a baby."

I won't tire you with the rest of that conversation. It raged back and forth between us like electricity arcing between two points. Sam was a woman obsessed, and nothing was going to turn her. That was why I gave in, in the end: it was nothing to do with her threats, though she probably thought it was; I simply knew that if I refused to help, she would find another way. And hazardous though the undertaking was, there are worse dangers out there for the unwary – and the innocent. I tried to warn her. She didn't refuse to listen, but she heard me out with a sullen, hard expression on her face, the expression of a rebellious child being lectured by a parent. And at the end she still pressed me to go on.

So I did it. I took up the tools I had sworn never

to use again, and waded back into the dark waters I had sworn never to re-enter. I wove the wish, and Samantha gave it life. I did my best to guide her, but in the end the only real advice I could give her was: be specific. Magic has an unpleasant way of catching up loose ends and weaving them into something un-looked-for, something unwanted. Something wrong. Afterwards she looked at me suspiciously, almost with contempt. I think she could hardly believe that anything so homely could work. But magic does not need an environment of squalor, beldames crouching over belching cauldrons, one-eyed black tomcats with ragged ears hissing from dark corners. Don't believe everything you read.

Two weeks later to the day she telephoned me. There was joy in her voice.

"- Purslane, it's worked! I've just done the test."

"Hello, Sam."

"- Is it really Robert's? Will it look like him?"

"As much as any child resembles its parents."

"- Thank you, thank you."

Remember…be specific.

Two months later on and she telephoned me again. This time she was in tears. I could hear the rage and pain in her voice when she spoke, like gravel crunching underfoot.

At first she was so choked up that she was incoherent.

"Samantha? What's wrong?"

"The baby…" More sobbing.

"What about the baby?"

"There is no baby." Voice rising: "You cheated me."

I gripped the receiver hard in my fingers and deliberately kept my voice calm.

"What do you mean, there's no baby? Did you miscarry?"

"No…. I went for a scan. There's no baby. There's nothing growing."

I thought about this for a moment, trying to understand what could be wrong. At last I said, "When you did the test – are you sure it was positive?"

There was a pause, and then I heard her laugh, shrilly. "Of course I'm sure. I did another one this morning, and it came up positive again. I'm still throwing up every morning. I have cravings for raspberries. But they did the scan and there's nothing there."

I sighed. ""Sam, what did you wish for?"

"What do you mean?" Her voice was suspicious, uncertain.

"When we – you know. What exactly – and I

mean exactly – did you wish for?"

"I wished to be pregnant."

"You wished to bear a child?"

"I wished to be pregnant," she said again.

She must have heard me suck in my breath, because she immediately said, "What…?"

"You wished to be pregnant," I told her. "Ergo, you are pregnant. You're going to go on being pregnant. It wasn't specific enough, Sam. You needed to wish for the baby."

Of course, she wouldn't leave it at that. I could have undone what we did, she could have grieved, and recovered slowly, and got on with her life. Perhaps forgotten my brother, met someone else, had his babies. But she wouldn't give up. When I first saw her at the wedding, looking like one of those little figurines that they put on the top of wedding cakes, so blonde and pink-and-white, like a thing made of spun sugar, I never would have thought she would have such determination in her. There was nothing brittle about her. That pale beauty was just so much enamelling covering the hard metal underneath.

She came to see me again, and this time she didn't even bother pleading. She demanded. She threatened. She would peddle her secret – my secret – not only to my family but to anyone else who would listen. She would go to the press. She would go to the police.

Why did I agree? I didn't think for a moment that the press, the police, or anyone outside our family would believe her. They would think her accusations were the ravings of a woman driven outside the boundaries of normality by grief. Even my parents would probably turn a deaf ear to her story. They – most particularly my father – have a prodigious talent for ignoring what they would prefer not to know about.

And I didn't particularly like Sam. She was threatening me. She alternated between rage and storms of tears. Even if my brother had lived, I doubt we would ever have been close. In normal circumstances she would have been my polar opposite, the princess who is as good as she is beautiful. Still, I pitied her from the bottom of my heart. And she had been my brother's wife. Robert had loved her.

I did try to make her see reason.

"Robert's been dead nearly four months," I pointed out. "No-one's going to believe the child is his if you get pregnant now."

She stared back at me, mutinously.

"I'll tell everyone it was IVF, that we'd agreed to it

beforehand, in case anything ever happened to him. I'll tell them they made the preparations the week he was in hospital in the coma."

She had it all worked out. I think as well that she had gone beyond the point of caring what anyone else thought. Her grief for Robert, the wreck of her hopes, had hardened into a sharp point, and all the pressure was on this one theme. She had to have a baby.

I told her about the pitfalls, and she ignored them, like a drunk meandering carelessly through a minefield. I told her that this was a much more serious thing than before; Robert had been dead much longer. Before, it had been a matter of tweaking circumstances; she could so easily have been in the early weeks of pregnancy when Robert died. It was not so very difficult for it to be so. But now…

"There are limits to what I can do," I told her.

"Limits?" she said, uncomprehendingly.

"Magic has its rules, too," I said. "There are things you have to be aware of. Like being very, very careful what you wish for. Sometimes it can give you the precise thing you asked for, but it won't be the way you wanted it to be."

"Like wishing to be pregnant," she said, dully.

"Yes. You must be specific. Very specific. But

Sam…"

"Yes?" She glanced up at me, her eyes narrowed, waiting to see whether I would refuse to help.

"I can make magic, but I can't perform miracles."

"What are you saying?" Had her voice always been that hard? "Can I have my baby?"

"Yes." I saw her sag in visible relief. "But Sam – having Robert's baby, that isn't something that can be in anyone else's reality. Robert has been dead for four months. I can't change the world, I can't change the way everyone else experiences it. They can't know – not ever. I can only do this for you. Just for you."

She nodded silently, and I thought that she understood.

This time Sam didn't go for her twelve-week scan. No notes, no tests, no blood-pressure readings. She said it was because she didn't want anyone interfering, but I think it was really because she was afraid. Afraid that the scan would show an empty womb again, that she would have been cheated a second time. But all the signs were good: she threw up every morning for three months, and then settled down and began to bloom like an old-fashioned tea rose. Her waistline swelled and her face acquired that soft look which sometimes accompanies pregnancy. When she was about six months along, she felt the baby kicking. I had to hear about all of it, of course. Having elected to dispense with the doctors, she treated me as a counsellor, a practitioner, a confidante. The threats and demands were all forgotten.

She went into labour on the last day of April, a little earlier than expected – although it was hard to be exact, given the circumstances. After the pains began, she telephoned me, and then an ambulance. She had come this far without the aid of the medical profession, but the baby was going to be born in hospital. She was determined to give it the best possible start in life, to take no risks. Her mother was in the delivery room with her. I waited in a visitors' room, making myself as unobtrusive as possible. The baby was born as night fell. I felt the atmosphere change, as though the air pressure had dropped, and stepped into to the corridor. Along the passageway a commotion was going on. White-coated staff were rushing in and out. Someone was wheeling in equipment on a trolley, moving so quickly that the apparatus rattled. Rubber soles squealed on the linoleum floor. Above it all, I heard someone scream.

The baby was born dead. A perfect little boy, waxen and still. There was nothing that could be done, no resuscitation, no miracle injection. The doctors tried, but it was obvious from the beginning that it was hopeless. The screaming was Sam's mother. I peered around the door briefly, unnoticed in the commotion, and caught a momentary glimpse of Sam herself, lying half-propped up on the pillows. She was smiling beatifically, like a blonde angel. Her arms encircled – nothing.

Sam never went home. Her family, who arrived en masse to comfort her, found instead a woman apparently in the rosy throes of new motherhood. She smiled, and coo'ed, and offered her breast to an infant that no-one else could see. The sight of their daughter singing to an invisible child made Sam's parents scurry off to find a consultant. Terms like post-partum psychosis were murmured out of Sam's hearing, not that she would have taken any notice. She was too wrapped up in her new role as mother. Curiously enough, she continued to lactate long after the milk should have dried up. She was hastily moved into a private room whilst the family and the medical staff tried to decide what to do with her. Since the baby was dead, they could hardly put her into the special unit for mothers with post-natal psychological problems. Whilst the whispering went on, Sam continued to occupy herself with her child. She asked her parents to bring her things – tiny clothes, nappies, a rattle. They looked at her with horror. Sam seemed annoyed that her parents were not fulfilling their roles as grandparents, but otherwise she was unmoved. At last she was sectioned.

I visit her sometimes. I'm the only one from our family who does so. My mother finds it too painful – the child everyone thought Sam was having would have been her grandson, after all. My father simply buries himself deeper inside his seemingly boundless facility for ignoring what is unpleasant. Sam's name never passes his lips, and Robert's does very rarely. But I go sometimes and sit with her for an hour. The staff tell me that my visits are the only ones she seems to enjoy, the only ones which touch her. They think it is because my presence soothes her; I always stay calm, whereas Sam's family tend to become emotional. But I know it's nothing to do with that. Sam likes my visits because I am the only one who can see her baby.

I can't see him all the time; only his mother can do that. But I catch glimpses. Sometimes I see him for the whole hour I am there, sometimes not at all. Sam loves it when she knows I see him; she loves to show him off.

"Look at the lady, Robbie," she says, smiling happily as she turns him to face me. My heart is always struck cold at these times. Robbie looks at me, unsmilingly, and gazing into his empty eyes is like looking into the entrance of a dark cave. You might think you see life within, but all you are really seeing is the dancing of reflected light on the walls, the encrusted dripping of stalactites. Everything is dead.

I wish I had made the warnings clearer; I wish I had known beforehand. I told her magic has its limits, its rules. I should have told her that only God can make a soul.

I still visit her. That is my penance.

Minnow Slough

K. Woo

Eldon's face shone deathly white as he slowly staggered through the door. Conversations and dart games ceased simultaneously as if by command. Every eye in the shabby flyspecked bar watched his slow progress across the floor to the stools. He no sooner sat down than his head collapsed into his hands.

"Eldon. Eldon, what's wrong with you?" Pops asked as he limped through his own cigar smoke towards the shaken man. The baldhead with a three-day-old gray beard thrust forward. "Eldon, you look like a haint dun got hold of you."

Eldon rubbed his hands up his face, over his head and down to his shoulders. He sat up and took a deep breath of the stale smoke ridden air. His all too white eyes focused on Pops. "My damn truck broke down again."

"Hell boy. My truck breaks down all the damn time. It don't ever make me look like that." Pops pointed to Eldon's reflection in the mirror behind the bar. Eldon peered through decades of dirt, smoke and grime on the glass to see the face of a man terrified within an inch of his life.

"I broke down at the end of Minnow Slough, over by the path and Fletcher Road," Eldon explained. "I figured I'd just cut through the path and save myself about three miles of walking."

"Eldon, you're a damn fool. You know there's a full moon out tonight." Pops looked at Eldon like he was an idiot that had to be told the stove was hot on a daily basis. He set a beer in front of the distressed man. Eldon picked it up and took a swallow. He closed his eyes and drew a deep breath. A little color dared to creep back into his face.

"What kinda boogie man story you telling over here Eldon?" The question came from a small group of men being drawn to the end of the bar. They all obviously had a touch or four to drink so far, their clothing already loose and their faces already red.

"I'm telling you. I've never been so scared in all my life," Eldon said as he turned the crusty bar stool to face the men as they gathered round. Pops stood by patiently, waiting for the whole story. Eldon looked around and knew he had a tale to tell. He took a deep breath and sighed.

"Alright. Look, I'm headed over here from the plant. I had to work late tonight. The damn truck starts loosing power right after I turn off on Fletcher."

"You check the fuel filter?" one of the patrons offered.

Pops swung a dish rag at the helpful one and reprimanded, "Shut up fool. Let's hear the whole story first then we can play shade tree mechanic."

The group laughed and jostled Pops' victim. Eldon took a long draw from his glass. He exhaled heavily. Everyone got quiet.

"I got that piece of junk off the road. It won't do a thing, so figure I'll just walk on around here and get someone to come help me. Well, I walked a bit and I didn't see anyone on the road. I got to the head of the path and I figured I'd save myself some shoe leather. I'd just cut across and we could drive back around."

Eldon looked around as he talked. Everyone in the place hung on his every word and looked straight at him. He nervously took another sip for courage.

"I know the slough is supposed to be haunted or cursed or whatever but no one believes in that stuff anymore. So, I got about half way through, you know, over by the bridge. That's when I started hearing stuff in there. I mean something big got real close." Eldon started pointing and waving his hands around for emphasis as he spoke.

"What was it?" the boldest and drunkest of the crowd, Bret, had to ask.

Eldon looked Bret dead in the eye as he answered his question, "I honest to God don't know. I started feeling all funny, like I was being watched. The faster I walked, the scareder I got." Eldon shivered at the next thought. "Then I started feeling things like they was touching me. Man, that was when I had enough. I took out running. I don't know what it was and I was not about to find out. I didn't stop running till I got here."

Pops broke the ensuing moment of silence. "Well that will learn ya to stay out of that slough during a full moon. That place has been touched by a devil. That's what my granddad told me and I still believe him."

Bret started laughing. He slapped the top of the bar, turned around to check the look on everyone's faces and busted out louder. He took a couple of steps and stopped.

"Y'all ain't nothing but a bunch of scared old women." He raised his voice for effect. "Oh, don't go down by the swamp under a full moon or the boogie man will getcha. I got over that bs when I was a kid." Bret pointed wildly towards the door. "There ain't nothing out there but deer, turtles and snakes."

"Bret, I'm telling you. There's something out there that just ain't right." Eldon had the look of a believer as he spoke. "I know. I was just out there."

Bret thought about that for a minute. He turned to the room in general and announced, "I got fifty says I will walk over to Eldon's truck and I'll take the path."

"Bret, your alligator mouth is about to overload your butterfly butt." Pops gave him a knowing look to go with the words.

One of the group asked, "If you come running out of there like a woman at either end of that path, you lose?"

"You got yourself a bet," Bret crowed proudly.

Eldon slid down the bar with Pops while the rest of the patrons worked out their bets and conditions. Both men looked back at the group and shook their heads sadly.

"Let them get it all out of their systems and I will run ya around to get your truck," Pops said quietly to Eldon. He nodded and smiled in return.

The ruckus died down at the end of the bar far

too soon for the expedition to have been forgotten. The entire group headed down to the end where Pops and Eldon had tried to escape. They had the look of men drunk on their own daring among other spirits.

"Ok, Pops, hand over Bouncer and let's get on with it," Bret announced loudly over the noise of his followers. He clearly enjoyed the attention and intended to make the most of it.

"Bouncer stays under the bar where it belongs," Pops responded indignantly. He stared back into Bret's face.

"Come on Pops. I need it for snakes out there. Besides, if I ain't here, who you gunna use it on?" Bret laughed at his own joke while the rest of the crowd laughed at him. Everyone looked expectantly at Pops. Now, he had to either one up Bret or hand over Bouncer. He decided to do both.

"Well, you got a point there. You just remember that ol' Bouncer is softer than your head. So you be careful not to get either one of them broke." Pops laid an ancient solid wood baseball bat on the counter and rolled it across the bar to Bret. Bret snatched it up and held it over his head like a trophy.

"Alright boys, lets go." Bret announced as he strode towards the door. The throng followed him out. Eldon looked up at Pops and shook his head sadly from side to side.

"You know, Pops, this ain't gunna be nothing but trouble. That damn fool is just asking for it." Eldon looked at Pops as he spoke. He started to feel responsible for this mess. All he wanted to do was get the story off his chest, have a beer, get his truck and go home. Now, it had just got worse. Nothing quite like a pack of good old boys liquored up and loose in a swamp to make a bad night longer. At least they would not have to go far. The head of the path through Minnow Slough started right across the street.

Pops could see the haunted look that still held sway in Eldon's eyes. The boys were about to stir up something they really did not want to tangle with and there was nothing either one of them could do about it. Pops looked around his now empty place and sighed, "Come on Eldon. Let's go see what these damn fools are gunna do."

Both men walked slowly out the door. The warm night air greeted them. To Eldon, the night air still held the stench of fear. The full moon above told Pops everything he needed to know. People do crazy stuff under a full moon. It is called lunacy for a reason. They both watched as money got waved about and bets got placed. Some of the men received the assignment to stay on this end of the path to make sure Bret did not double back and sneak out. The rest are to drive around and wait at the other end. Pops and Eldon just sat down at the end of the deck. This looked far enough for them.

Bret, waving Bouncer over his head, started jogging down the path into the darkness of the slough with only the moon to light his way. As soon as he faded into the obscurity of the trail, it occurred to the ones left to watch that there really was not much to do. They began wandering loosely back across the road to where Pops and Eldon sat. Cigarettes lit, the waiting officially began. A few minutes later, several vehicles arrived at the other end of the path. They all pulled off to the side of the road. The other half of the stakeholders in Bret's adventure got out and milled around. There is a funny thing about getting a group all wound up. It is usually followed by a lot of waiting with nothing else to do.

Bret quit jogging as soon as he rounded the first bend and he could no longer be seen. He patted his pockets as he walked and found his cigarettes. Tucking Bouncer under his arm he managed to get one lit. He figured it would take him less than an hour to walk across the slough. That should be enough time to think up something to do to those idiots waiting for him. Once they had been scared real good, it would be time for all of them to go do something to the group waiting at Pops. He began letting the bat swing loosely back and forth in his hand as he walked and smoked.

He dropped the butt and stepped on it. No reason to start a fire tonight. Bret patted his back pocket and found his backup courage supply. He pulled out the classic metal flask and held it up in front of him and smiled. He unscrewed the cap and took a swig. That hit the spot. A little liquid courage never hurt.

The sounds of water on both sides of the path dominated the night's persistent clatter. Here and there, he would hear the gentle splash of the minnows that gave this place its name or the animals that fed on them. He looked up at the moon as he walked. It hung directly overhead. It appeared unusually massive for this time of night. The warm moist air made it appear almost three dimensional. If he tried, he thought he could see the curve of its surface. Then again, it could all just be the drink. Bret kept walking.

The initial excitement and bravado wore off fairly quickly. Instead of sitting at a table with a nice cold one, he now tromped through this cursed swamp. He smiled at the thought of the beer money this little hike would put in his pocket. A bunch of grown men acting like old women. Afraid of a full moon and a little tall grass, they ought to be ashamed of themselves. Every so often, small animals scurried away from in front of him. From the sound of things, they were shocked to be meeting a human out here at this time of night.

Bret started to sweat. All the drinking tonight did not making this hike any easier. He lit another cigarette as he walked. He swatted Bouncer at the grass tops and tall weeds as he passed. In spite of the time of night, he could see the path just fine, the full moon lit the way. The leaves and grass rustled softly under his feet. He grew warm from the walk and the cloying night air hung on him.

He would soon be approaching the old wood bridge that spanned the main body of open water. So far, he had not seen any snakes or much of anything else larger than a field mouse. He had heard plenty of stuff getting away from him as fast as it could. A slight breeze finally started giving him some relief from the dank night air. The breeze tugged lightly at his hair and clothes.

The bridge loomed out of the darkness as he kept

walking. This meant he had already covered over half the way to his waiting entourage. Just a little further and he would be counting his money. Bret stopped and took a big swig from his liquid courage supply. He wiped his lips and put the flask away. He stepped up on to the first wooden plank. His footstep echoed off the water flowing below. Bret's heavy steps magnified as he mounted the structure. At the center of the bridge he stopped, leaned on the guardrail, and looked out across the tall grasses and water. The moon shone brightly casting deep shadows everywhere he looked. He lit another ciga-rette and smoked it staring out across the nocturnal landscape.

"Ain't nothing to it you bunch of chickens." Bret shouted triumphantly to every one who could not hear him. He flicked his latest cigarette butt off into the water.

Just as he heard the plop then fizzle of the burn-ing tobacco, water burst up out of the depth of the shadows. Bret's heart leapt in his chest. He nearly fell over backwards as the spray hit his face. Bouncer rattled to the wooden slats that made up the bridge. The sound of wood striking wood echoed across the wetland. Bret scrambled for the bat. Loud thuds came back from under the bridge as he stumbled and reached.

Bret's fingers closed around the circular old wood. He sprang to his feet. More deep sounds hit him from under the bridge. Bret dashed forward. His head flung from side to side. His eyes flew wide open to see as well as he could in the dark shadows. Something ethereally cool wiped slightly across his face. He spun but couldn't see anything. His foot caught and he sprawled to the dirt. This time, he held onto the bat for dear life. He rolled to his back and held Bouncer over himself like a talisman against evil. His heart pounded and his breathing labored. With wild eyes, he looked around for what tripped him. Nothing at his feet, nothing more than the first plank of wood that began the bridge.

Bret pulled himself back up to his feet. He felt a slight tug on his shirt behind him. He spun swinging the bat with deadly force. Bouncer found only air. He spun back the other way. He had seen, out of the corner of his eye, something move. There just behind him. He swung again. Again, he found only the deep nocturnal shadows cast under the full moon. Bret could hear his heartbeat in his ears now. His breathing came like a bellows. Sweat literally poured off him. The shadows moved again in the corner of his eye. He swung and swung again. Just as he would stop one swing, he would feel a little tug on his hair. He would swing back. Nothing to connect with but he'd feel a slight tug at his shirt. Time and time again he fought the empty black air. He knew something lurked there. He just couldn't get a piece of it. If it ever slowed down, he would make it pay. It rustled on this side. It tugged on that side. It never moved in front of him. It was always just in the corner of his eye or behind him. He had to keep swinging to keep it off of him.

Bret could hardly stand, his hands numb, his arms made of lead. It still skulked there in the edge of his vision. His eyes, wide with panic, could still see the shifting shadows. He could still feel the terrible teasing tugs. His chest rose and fell as he desperately fought the gloom for air. Finally, he could hear its footsteps. It thought it could sneak up on him, wrong. He could hear it coming. He could see its glow through the tall grasses. The shadows leapt in front of his eyes in a terrible dance. Bret steeled himself for one last round.

The thing's terrible eyes came into view, huge and horrible. Three feet off the ground and six feet apart they floated. It knew his name. He heard it call his name, softly at first, but it kept getting louder and louder. Over and over it called him. It crept closer.

Bret knew he could never take it now. It had worn him down and it came for him. He looked up at the full moon and watched it spin above him. The end had come.

Just on the far side of the bridge, Pops and Eldon saw Bret crumpled on the ground. They had been the only ones brave enough to walk through the path when Bret had not appeared on the other side. Pops had a pair of good lanterns he kept in the bar in case the lights went out. They lit the path through the slough. Bret still breathed but that was about all they could say for him. He lay there covered in dirt and sweat. They rolled him over. They couldn't see any blood anywhere.

Eldon finally spoke. "Pops, what happened to him?"

"Well, near as I can figure, you had sense enough to run when a devil touched you. This fool waited to get slapped down."

About the Authors

Nick Aires (*A Fool And His Honey*) is an L. Ron Hubbard Writers of the Future finalist, and the co-author of the action-packed fantasy novel *Judgement Day* (Five Star, 2005). He's published dozens of stories in anthologies, magazines, and online. Nick's also the coeditor of *Fantasy Readers Wanted—Apply Within*.

Barry Baldwin (*If I Had A Hundred Tongues*) lives in Calgary, Alberta, where he served as Professor of Classics at the University of Calgary. Since his retirement in 1997, he has reinvented himself as a freelance magazine/newspaper writer.

Stanley T. Evans (*Black Water Bayou*) is a true fan of all things arcane. Mr. Evans' short stories have been feautred in several anthologies.

James Ferris (*Black Mary*) is currently a resident of Memphis, Tennessee. Mr. Ferris works as a computer network administrator and has a deep interest in all things magical.

Allan Gilbreath (*Lepus Europaeus*) is an experienced writer in both fiction and non-fiction. Mr. Gilbreath's work has appeared in numerous anthologies, magazines, and online features.

Nicholas Knight (*In The Name of Desdemonia*) fiction can be found in *Dead Winter, Futures Mysterious Anthology Magazine*, H.P. Lovecraft's *Magazine of Horror, Mystery In Mind, Open Space*, and the back of IDW comics, among other publications.

Lori Rapti (*Cleanup On Aisle Seven*) is originally from New Jersey and now residing in the South. Ms. Osif provides a very unique point of view for story telling.

Rob Rosen (*The Wish*) lives, loves, and works in San Francisco, California. His first novel, *Sparkle*, was published in 2001, and his short stories appear regularly on literary Web sites and in print anthologies and magazines.

K. Woo (*Minnow Slough*) is a computer programmer from Visckburg, Mississippi with a deep love of books and bookstores.

Donna L. Zeller (*Loves Magic*) writes fiction and non-fiction from Harrisburg, Pennsylvania. Her first novel, *Nalla's Attic Auction*, is a mystery geared toward young adults. A second young-adult novel, *The Mystery Trip*, is scheduled for publication in 2006.

Kathleen McCarthy (*The Crystal*)
Helen Grant (*The Rules of Magic*)
Mark Deloy (*Encounter*)
Albert Coelho (*Heirlooms*)
Jeannie Mobley (*In The Headlights*)
Louise Yeiser (*My Little Elves*)

Printed in the United States
38121LVS00001B/4-27